The Best Doctor in Town

A Tall Tale of the Hills

AMELIA TOWNSEND

The Best Doctor in Town
A Tall Tale from the Hills
Amelia Townsend

Published September 2019
Little Creek Books
Imprint of Jan-Carol Publishing, Inc.

Front Cover Design: Powell Valley News, Josh Watson—Graphic Designer

ISBN: 978-1-950895-17-5
Library of Congress Control Number: 2019949605

You may contact the publisher:
Jan-Carol Publishing, Inc.
PO Box 701
Johnson City, TN 37605
publisher@jancarolpublishing.com
jancarolpublishing.com

To my mother, Ruby, and the best
storytelling friend a girl could ask for—
the late, incomparable Dink E. Shakleford.

Acknowledgments

To all the officers of the courts and individuals who answered countless questions, the librarians who tracked down unending source materials, the hospital staff and family members who work in healthcare who explained processes and procedures.

To the people of my beloved Virginia Mountains, whose ability to endure seemingly insurmountable challenges with unbroken faith and grace inspired the characters.

To the Board of Directors, actors, crew, and supporters of Shoestring Theatre Company, who brought this story to life as a stage play.

To Dr. Victoria Molnar Weiss, FVAO, who is the former president of the Board of Remote Area Medical, and to all the volunteers and staff of RAM whose relentless pursuit of providing health care for those who need it most inspired this story.

CHAPTER 1

Patient Love

Lying among the crumpled sheets on a hospital bed, the dying man gasped for air. Stretching a trembling hand into the air above him, Joe Blevins struggled to focus his clouded eyes on the familiar face of the smiling, be-speckled doctor peering down toward him. The words came hard, pushing through gasps of air.

"Please. Doc Briggs. Help. Me. I. Have. Never. Been. Sick. I am only 63 years old." His chest heaved, and with each exhale, the haggard face deflated.

With a consoling pat on Joe's shoulder, Dr. Nicholas "Briggs" Oxenbriggs slowly increased the drip on the IV that traced down to the man's withered arm.

"Joe, I love you. You are my favorite patient. I will take good care of you, my friend, good care."

Dr. Oxenbriggs pulled a slender syringe from the breast pocket of his crisp, white hospital jacket, and in one calming move, he pushed the clear contents of the cylinder into a port on the IV line. He carefully lowered Joe's extended arm to his side. "It's okay, Joe. This will help. I assure you. I love you."

Briggs stepped back, cocked his head from side to side, watching like a cat waiting for a trapped mouse to move. Joe struggled, gasped, shuddered, then finally convulsed and fell backward. Silent. Dr. Oxenbriggs leaned over his now dead patient, raised Joe's left hand, and removed the diamond-studded ring from his limp pinky finger. Studying it for a moment, Dr. Oxenbriggs dropped the glittering hoop into the breast pocket on his lab coat. For a moment, the tall, muscular doctor with greying salt and pepper hair rubbed his patient's placid face, and then with a sigh, he said, "I loved you, Joe, and you are much better off now."

Dr. Oxenbriggs patted the ring resting in his jacket pocket. "I will always have you with me," he whispered.

Leisurely, he pulled the emergency call button, then yelled urgently into the speaker.

"Code Black. Code Black. This is Dr. Oxenbriggs. Code Black. STAT!"

Almost instantaneously, the emergency team of nurses, assistants, and medical residents shoved into the room at the Lone Mountain Medical Center in Big Stone Gap, Virginia. They found Dr. Briggs frantically pressing his hands into the dead man's chest, performing CPR on the lifeless body of Joe Blevins.

"Hurry! I'm losing him. Joe! Joe! Stay with me!" Dr. Oxenbriggs ordered the bevy of nurses, medical residents, and assistants who quickly moved into action. No one seemed to notice that the heart monitors had long-since stopped beeping.

After a while, Briggs said softly, "Call it." Another voice responded, "Time of death, o-eight-hundred."

Briggs stood, staring at the body of the man who had been very much alive just a few moments before. He rushed forward and gathered Joe's body into his strong arms. He wept. "Joe, you cannot be gone."

Several members of the team tried to pull the doctor back, but he jerked away. Soon, he reluctantly and gently laid the body onto the bed. Briggs shook his head, wiped his face, straightened his lab coat, and wiped a single tear from his cheek.

"I've done all I could, all I could. He was my favorite patient. Can someone call the family, please?"

Two of the medical assistants reached out to console Dr. Oxenbriggs, but he jerked away from their touch, turning to rest his hands on their shoulders instead. "No need. No need. I'm more concerned about Joe and his family," Briggs choked back a sob and moved toward the door. Before he pushed out into the hallway, he turned to one of the residents.

"Sign the death certificate, please? I need to be alone for a moment."

All except one member of the team watched reverently as with one long sigh, the grand doctor strode out of the room into the bright bustle of the hospital corridor. Once out of view of the room, Dr. Oxenbriggs patted the breast pocket of his starched-white lab coat and smiled. "I loved you, Joe. You'll be with me always."

The doctor who hung back was Dr. Ash McKay, who did not give way to the worship of Dr. Oxenbriggs. He remained quietly standing in the darkest corner of the late Joe Blevins' hospital room, entertaining an uncomfortable, nagging suspicion. As chief resident and top Fellow in the Community Medical Care Program that Dr. Oxenbriggs headed at Lone Mountain, McKay often stood alongside Briggs when he saw patients. McKay had been the first to respond last week when they lost another elderly patient.

In that case as well, when the team responded to Dr. Oxenbriggs' call for help, they found the great physician frantically performing CPR on Mrs. Sarah Madison. In what was an almost identical display, Dr. Oxenbriggs had struggled heroically to will the elderly woman back to life. He had sobbed that he loved her. He mourned that he had lost his favorite patient. He stood over the body and wiped away tears. The scene was all too similar for the analytical Dr. McKay. He had no evidence, but the voices telling McKay something was wrong roared rather than whispered.

Last week's patient was a 77 year-old mother and grand-mother, Sarah Madison. She had raised 10 children alone in the tiny community of Josephine, just outside Norton, Virginia. Set in the shadows of the Blue Ridge Mountain chain that enveloped most of Wise County, Josephine had once been a thriving train stop with some homes, a church, a store, a post office, and even a one-roomed school. By the time Sarah found the place, all that remained were the fading remnants of the one-roomed schoolhouse, the church, and a limestone train depot that stood defiantly on the edge of the weedy, rusted railroad tracks.

What most people thought of as abandoned, Sarah saw as a home for herself and the children. Her husband died in a mining accident in 1960. The union benefits helped, but they did not put a roof over Sarah's head, and the money didn't buy food for the table. Sarah couldn't find work in those days. She had been walking home to the rented house up in the holler when she passed by the tiny sign that said, "Josephine."

Something drew her to the overgrown site. She walked along the remnants of the dirt road that led to the train station. The weeds dragged against her skirt. The briars nicked her legs. Once, she looked at the thicket surrounding her and thought about snakes. Copperheads were not uncommon, and this was the season for them. She stepped more carefully, making her way to the train station, which still stood defiantly as if it were a sentry guarding the site against the encroaching weeds and overgrowth. Sarah peeked inside the broken glass. Something scurried along the floor. That didn't scare her. From what she could see, the structure appeared sound. Sarah stepped back and scanned the entire area.

It needed work. She was not afraid of that. She and her children could turn this place into a home. She walked around, envisioning a future here. She stooped down and picked up a handful of dirt. The soil felt silky and rich. Good for corn. Where weeds and saplings grew, Sarah saw rows of green corn bending softly to a gentle wind. Where green kudzu covered the train station, Sarah saw a clean limestone home with a red door and grey front porch. Where there stood nothing more than emptiness, Sarah saw a manicured lawn filled with the delightful laughs of children—her children.

She didn't ask anyone if she could move into Josephine. Sarah figured that it had long ago been abandoned, so no one cared. She was almost right. For the next several years, Sarah and her children cleared the land together, rebuilt the floor in the train station, planted a garden, and eventually bought a cow and some chickens. They created a fence around the old store and turned it into a milking barn and chicken coop. She made this once ghostly place a true home that protected and loved Sarah and her family for nearly 50 years.

After she and her children had been in Josephine for

nearly a decade, they were visited by a man who claimed that he owned the property. He told Sarah that she would either have to pay rent or leave. Normally suspicious of authorities and afraid of losing her only home, Sarah asked for some time to think about her options. The man gave her one week.

Sarah's oldest son, who was now in his 20's and preparing to go into the military, offered to talk to his recruiting officer in Kingsport. That turned out to be the best idea in the universe as far as Sarah and her family were concerned. The recruiting officer guided Sarah's son to the court records. Through that, he learned that the man was lying. The land had been abandoned years ago. If Sarah worked with the county to pay the back taxes, she would own the land outright. It took another five years, and with the help of her now grown son and daughter, Sarah and her family earned the deed to the land.

Until a fall forced her to hobble about on crutches, Sarah Madison kept Josephine alive for a growing family that now included a dozen grandchildren and couple of great grandchildren.

"Strong mountain grit," her oldest daughter had described her mother. "Shc had to do all the repairs, raised us, and worked as the cook in the elementary school down in Big Stone Gap to bring in a little money."

Probably because of her hard-scrabble life, Sarah never

suffered the diseases common to most of her mountain neighbors—heart disease, diabetes, high blood pressure, or depression. Yet, within a month after that short fall inside her home sent her to the hospital, Sarah began to hallucinate. She suffered two minor strokes, convulsions, became very forgetful, and finally, she could not swallow. Food particles trickled into her lungs, and in the end, the once vibrant woman lay nearly motionless in a hospital bed—a heap of heaving bones and skin. She died in a room at Lone Mountain Medical Center while all her children and grandchildren had gone home to rest.

Even the passionate skills of Dr. "Briggs" Oxenbriggs had failed, and the staff's admiration of Briggs solidified when they witnessed him surreptitiously wiping a tear outside Sarah's hospital room.

Briggs counseled Ash following Sarah's death. "Sometimes the elderly person innately knows death is coming and does not want their family to live with those memories. Therefore, the dying person somehow summons the will to pass when none of their loved ones are present. You do all you can and then know people like Sarah are at peace—out of the pain, the struggle, the hurt."

McKay didn't subscribe to that theory. He considered himself a scientist whose primary area of research was the human body. He had little faith in anecdotal or empirical evidence—only that which could be proven, and preferably after double-blind, peer-reviewed research studies to verify the results.

Now, recalling the two scenes, a stubborn hunch protruded from the deep recesses of Ash's analytical mind. He tried to push the idea out—negate it because there was no factual basis. Yet, the notion would not abate. Could it be that his boss, his mentor, his reason for choosing the Community Medical Care Program, the unrivaled Dr. Nicholas "Briggs" Oxenbriggs had just staged some grand emotional pageant for his staff to witness? But to what purpose? There was no evidence of anything other than the fact that Dr. Oxenbriggs had worked valiantly to save two patients. All Ash had was a weird, unwanted thought that he willed himself to ignore.

Meanwhile, in another hospital room down the hallway, Eliot West paced in front of the hospital bed, where his father, Ira, sat and watched. Beside him sat Eliot's mother, Etta, gently holding Ira's hand. She kept a keen eye on her husband for any signs of another stroke. Meanwhile, Eliot could not be still. In his mid-thirties, Eliot's compact, muscular frame looked more like that of a body builder than a police officer.

"Son," Ira said, "Please sit down."

"Dad," Eliot's raspy voice contradicted his nervous movements. "We've been waiting a long time since they brought you up here from the ER."

As he moved, the black handle of his handgun jutted out beneath his brown leather jacket. Ira, whose eagle eyes never missed a thing, saw the weapon.

"Son, how did you get that gun in here? There are rules, even for cops, you know," Ira chided. A wry smile crossed Ira's pale face. He was an older, greyer, and slightly thinner version of his son. "But sit down, please. You're going to cause me to have a stroke." Ira smiled broadly.

"You're not funny." Shaking his head of shoulder-length brown hair and pushing his eye glasses back onto the top of his head, Eliot flopped into the black recliner across from the hospital bed. He could not stop fidgeting, glancing from the door to the room and back to his father.

"May as well laugh," Ira spread his free arm and kissed Etta on the head. "After all, laughter," he began, and Etta and Eliot chimed in.

"...is the best medicine."

"Okay, you win, Dad," Eliot stretched to his full height and forced himself to sit still.

Looking to Etta, Ira warned her. "Mamma, I will be home in time, so don't you even think about packing that truck by yourself."

Petite, with short, dark hair and a round, pug-nosed face and two deep, brown eyes, Etta West gave her husband a look of astonished anger. "Ira, we are not going to Michigan. I've already called your brother to tell him."

She stood beside the bed, stretching to her full five-foot-five height, and began to fluff Ira's pillows, moving him as necessary. Smiling all the while, he accommodated her fussing over him.

"Etta, honey, this was a mild stroke. As you can see, I'm perfectly fine, and I want to see my brother. With that cancer he has, there isn't much time."

Etta adjusted the white sheets and soft, blue blanket around her cheerfully-compliant husband. Over their 40 years of marriage, Ira had come to one conclusion: Etta wins every time. He loved her so much that he never wanted to be the cause of any pain or distress for her. Theirs had been a relationship that defined the word "cherish." Eliot watched them for a long moment, wishing his own marriage had been more like his parents, trying to discern what they did right and what he failed to do.

He had met his wife, Rhett, in Knoxville the first year he had worked for the city police department there. As a rookie patrol officer, Eliot put in long hours, night shifts, and went to school so he could advance in his career. Rhett had been a rock of support, and Eliot thought he was providing the same love and security for her.

Yet, there was never enough money, never enough time for one another. Rhett rarely complained, but Eliot saw the pained looks when she had to make do with an old dress to wear to her sister's wedding. He felt guilty when he could not buy a nice gift or take her to a special restaurant for their anniversary. He wanted to see Rhett smile, to hear her laugh, and to be as joyful as she had been in the beginning of their love. Eliot said he owed her that much and more. He wanted to cherish Rhett in the same way he saw his parents love one another. Eliot desperately sought a means to bring their love to life again. The scheme he landed upon seemed foolproof. It didn't seem like a crime at all. Take the drugs and illegal booze confiscated and used as evidence in court cases and sell it back to the criminals. It was nearly a perfect crime. Nearly.

Eliot's thoughts were broken when the hospital room door swung wide and Dr. Oxenbriggs strode in. Ira sat up straighter. Etta moved toward the tall, bespectacled doctor and extended her hand.

"Doctor Oxenbriggs," she said with a tone of relief. "We're so glad you're here."

"Hey Briggs," Ira exclaimed. "Will you tell my warden and jailer here that I'm fine and we can go to Michigan next week?"

"Hello, Ira, Etta, Eliot. I must be in the wrong room. I'm supposed to be checking on a stroke patient," Dr. Oxenbriggs moved with grace, warmly caressing Etta's hand and then in seemingly one motion, grabbing Ira's outstretched hand.

"I tell you, I feel great," Ira said emphatically.

Etta shook her head and rolled her eyes. "Too great,

Dr. Oxenbriggs. He thinks we're driving to Detroit just as planned before all this."

While listening, Dr. Oxenbriggs examined Ira, checking his eyes with a light, looking into his ears, thumping on his back, and watching as Ira followed the doctor's gestures with his own hands. After a moment, the doctor stood back, folded his arms, and rubbed his chin.

"Well, Ira, you did have a mild stroke, and I want to admit you to the hospital for a couple of days run a few more tests. Then, assuming you keep progressing, you can go home," Dr. Oxenbriggs counseled.

Etta offered her husband and son a satisfied look and walked past Dr. Oxenbriggs to stand beside Ira, where she began adjusting his blanket and fluffing his pillows again. Her next words were interrupted by Dr. Ash McKay, who opened the door and stepped inside. Looking around apologetically, he quickly realized that Dr. Oxenbriggs was in the middle of a consultation.

"Oh, sorry. Dr. Oxenbriggs, room 112 needs you—as soon as you can, sir," Dr. McKay whispered.

Briggs smiled broadly, reaching out to welcome McKay. "Everyone, please meet Dr. Ash McKay. He is my chief resident. You will be seeing him from time to time. He's the best I've seen in years, and we are so fortunate to have him in our community medical program."

Everyone in the room smiled and nodded. Then, turning

his attention to Ira, Dr. Oxenbriggs walked to stand by the bed. He told the West family how he met Dr. McKay through the Remote Area Medical program and how so many young medical professionals were learning about the needs in Southwest Virginia through the RAM. Ash noticed that Dr. Oxenbriggs carefully avoided taking any credit for attracting the interns or for growing the community medical program that kept the best and brightest here after their graduation.

People who knew of Dr. Briggs' contributions to improving medical care for the people of this remote region would have said he was being unduly humble. At that very moment, Ash would have agreed with them. But a few short weeks later, he would find himself being the only dissenter in a town full of Briggs' disciples.

"Dr. McKay," Briggs proudly stated. 'I'd like you to meet my favorite patient, Ira West. He has had a mild stroke. Looks like he'll recover nicely. But he has some concerns about going on with his life and taking a planned trip. What would you tell him?"

This was a test, and Ash knew it, but he was less certain of the right answer. He knew from experience that a response that differed from what Dr. Oxenbriggs wanted could cost him. He felt everyone staring at him. The pressure increased.

"I would tell you, Mr. West, that Dr. Oxenbriggs is right.

Strokes are tricky. Consider this an ounce of prevention, and take all the time to recover," Ash hoped the sigh he released did not betray his anxiety.

After a moment, Briggs displayed that brilliant, approving smile Ash had come to know so well. He pulled up Ira's chart, scribbled a few notes, and placed it back into a holder on the foot of the bed. Eliot, who had been uncharacteristically silent, walked toward his father's bed, where he could look Ash McKay and Oxenbriggs straight in the eyes.

"If you're sure he will improve," Eliot stated.

"You father has an excellent prognosis," Ash McKay said.

"I can hear you," Ira West chimed in. "I'm still alive over here."

"Honey, don't be rude. Of course you are!" Etta West chastised her husband.

With a chuckle and pat on Ira's arm, Dr. Oxenbriggs swept out of the room. They watched him disappear into the hallway. Then, Dr. McKay picked up Ira's medical chart, studying the notes left by Dr. Oxenbriggs. Quickly glancing back at the door, McKay flipped through the pages, then furiously wrote down something on the top page. Although Etta and Ira did not notice, Eliot caught McKay's struggle to hide his reaction to whatever he had read in the chart. McKay slid the chart back into its slot.

"I'll be on duty through tonight and tomorrow. So, I'll

check on you later. I've added a couple of tests here, all routine—cannot be too careful. Doc Briggs is right. Strokes can be tricky," McKay tried to get out of the room before anyone could ask any questions, but Eliot confronted him.

"What kind of tests?"

Ash addressed his response to Ira, ignoring Eliot. "Just a couple of more in-depth ultrasound scans—to check the blood flow to your brain, Mr. West. I see they did the CT and a routine MRI when you came in through the ER. The carotid ultrasound will show us the carotid artery, which delivers blood to the brain. We just want to be sure there's no serious blockage. The second is like the MRI, and again, it gives us more detail about the blood flow to your brain."

Etta walked to face Ash McKay. "Are you sure we need all these tests? You won't be cutting on him, will you? Nothing invasive."

Dr. McKay shook his head, offering her what he hoped was a comforting smile.

"Mrs. West, there is no surgery, nothing invasive whatsoever. These tests provide more detail—help us understand what caused this incident and give us information to provide more effective treatment for your husband. Are we all in agreement to move ahead?" Ash waited for their nods of agreement as Eliot stood to leave.

"It seems we have two good doctors, so I'll head off. Mamma, want anything from the house? I know you won't go home. I can get it and get back before my shift tonight."

"You won't need anything, Mamma," Ira called out. "I'm going home real soon."

Dr. McKay hurried out of the room, hoping to avoid talking with Eliot in the hallway. He always hated that moment when a doctor was forced to talk to a member of the patient's family, especially when that family member was a skeptical police officer. Besides, Ash was in a hurry to look up some additional information on the medical protocol for stroke patients. While he knew each doctor had his or her own methods, something he read in Ira's treatment plan seemed out of the standard care. He had to get his information quickly—before Dr. Oxenbriggs realized he was not on the floor.

CHAPTER 2
Shadow of the Mountain

Even in the 21st century, the arrowhead corner of southwest Virginia remained a mystery to most people in the rest of the Commonwealth, and the world for that matter. When national news reporters called officials in Appalachia, their questions were loaded with assumptions. They could not pronounce the name of the beautiful mountain chain that surrounded, protected, and isolated southwest Virginia.

"I'm doing a story on Apple- LAY-cha," they would proudly announce, rarely correcting themselves, even after they were told, "It's Apple-LATCH-ah." Then came the questions. "Could you put me in touch with a coal miner who makes moonshine?" "How about the teens? Do they work in the mines in their summer jobs?" "Do people finish high school?"

"I am looking for someone who lives in a cabin without electricity, you know, living off the land in the backwoods." "Do you have any minorities here?"

Local people had grown accustomed to the lack of

understanding that because of coal, this area had attracted experienced miners from Europe, Northern Africa, and the Middle East who arrived with their language and culture in the early 20th century. As one local described the remote mountain area, "We're the melting pot of the melting pot."

But the outside world didn't know that. In fact, most people thought that Virginia ended somewhere past Roanoke along U.S. Interstate 81.

Ashwood McKay found that to be the case when he tried to explain to his classmates at Coastal Virginia Medical School that he would be going to Southwest Virginia.

"So, you're going to Roanoke?" Ash's friends asked, puzzled.

"No," Ash would slowly explain. "That's four hours east of where I am going, which is Big Stone Gap. It's a lovely little town atop a rolling mountain in the very tip of the state. The hospital has a great community medicine program, and the head guy is well-respected. I'd get to work directly with him and with the patients, and what's even better is that if I stay, all my student loans will be paid in five years."

"Where did you say you're going?"

"Big Stone Gap, Virginia. It's in the mountains. It's beautiful, very quaint. Lots of running trails and great fishing."

"Ahh," and with that, the bewildered friends would walk

away, still mulling over the same geographical mystery that prompted their initial question.

Ash found it amusing because he had been one of them just few years earlier, before he took the call from the program director of a national residency matching service, more commonly known simply as "the match." He turned to the registry because competition made acceptance into many residency programs nearly impossible.

Although community medicine had not been particularly high on his list when Ash began medical school four years earlier, the shortage of family medical doctors for small, rural communities ramped up a virtual race among medical facilities to see which one could provide the most incentives to prospective doctors who agreed to stay for four years after their residency was completed. For Ash, who was born and raised by a single mother in Upstate New York, this arrangement would pay for medical school. He jumped at the offer, and the response came almost immediately.

During his first year, Ash had been among a group of medical students who were hand-picked to spend a weekend in the isolated Virginia mountains, assisting more than 200 volunteer doctors, dentists, and nurses from across the country, providing essential triage care to the most desperately ill people Ash had ever seen. Part of the Remote Area Medical Volunteer Corp created by a former TV celebrity and adventurer, the program provided free medical and dental care to hopeless, desperate, and unnecessarily ill people who had no jobs, no insurance, and no way to afford regular trips to the doctors or receive preventive care of any sort.

Along with a few free health clinics scattered over the hilly miles of the mountains, this intense clinic treated the worst of the ill and patched others with tiny rays of hope. And for mountain people accustomed to hard times, a little hope was just enough.

The first year, Ash made the day-long drive only because the invitation came with a generous stipend and an extra paid day off to "experience the mountains." The local planning team scheduled scenic hikes, including Benge's Trail to the Cumberland Gap, and fishing in one of the pristine rivers that cut gullies through the rock. Other activities included walking tours of Big Stone Gap and a visit to the only four-star restaurant in the entire mountain region. Fresh air and sleep were Ash McKay's heroin. But then he saw the people, and a new addiction consumed him.

"How could so much desperation, pain, and poverty exist in a country so filled with wealth, resources, and compassion?" Ash had wondered. "Yet, how could these people be so hopeful, so friendly, and so resilient?"

The answer to Ash's question lay in the isolation of the mountains where people had to creatively develop their own resources to solve problems that would have failed others who were unaccustomed to facing such daily insurmountable odds. The time could be divided into before railroads and coal and after coal.

Prior to the coming of the railroads in the late 1860's, the area had been home to generations who built their own communities from existing resources. Mountain medicine, sturdy cabins, and living off the land sustained generations of whites and Native Americans alike. Then, the railroad came, and investors found in it the means to move the coal out of the mountains. After the Civil War, investors poured into the mountains. They found a rich vein of coal and men willing to work underground to bring it out. Yet, there were not enough men, so by the time of World War I, when the demand for coal to make steel soared, experienced miners had been recruited from across the globe. Hungarians, Italians, Africans, and Middle Easterners all created their own cultures and communities in the hollers and hills of Southwest Virginia and beyond. Diversity was a way of life here.

Back in the early 20th century and well into the 1950's, the phrase "King Coal" meant something. Warming homes, fueling the production of steel, building the cars, the war material, and turning these isolated mountains into bustling, international communities, the seam of black beneath the mountains built thriving communities. Places like Stonega, Roda, and Appalachia, Virginia boasted world-class medical care. With good incomes, people pumped money into the communities that were underpinned by the black gold, whose endless supply gushed from the dark recesses of the earth, down the conveyor belts, and onto train cars and barges on rivers and across the nation.

Underwritten by the mining companies to keep miners producing, then supported by the miners themselves through their union dues, good health care was readily accessible. Towns like Big Stone Gap and Appalachia became filled with shops, restaurants, furniture stores, doctors' offices, and their own bus systems. Smaller communities boasted stores, schools, churches, and their own doctors. Community clubs, sports teams, and civic organizations abounded. However, with each mine shutdown, a piece of each town withered and died, until all that remained were the stubborn, coal ash covered brick buildings - reminders of a way of life that no longer existed. Once again, the mountains were becoming as isolated, as misunderstood, and the people as distant from the rest of the world as they had been before coal.

When Ash McKay stretched and stood after the nearly day-long ride in his Toyota Prius to the Wise County Fairgrounds that first year, he thought perhaps he had taken a wrong turn and ended up in a third-world country. Set on a sprawling fairground site, the three-day annual clinic drew thousands of hurting people who hobbled on canes, limped on weak legs, gasped for a breath, or wrangled wheelchairs over the rocky terrain. They displayed great patience, for they had appeared hours before daylight, slumped in a long, single line that stretched the length of a football field. They spoke softly, greeting friends and reuniting with others they had not seen since the last clinic—rejoicing in their joint survival to this time and place. To the uninitiated, this convention of last resort appeared peaceful and happy, but that was the outward demeanor of a people long-steeped in suffering and well-versed in surviving circumstances so dire, those with lesser strength of countenance would have crumbled.

It was during that first visit to the Remote Area Medical Clinic, or RAM, that Ash heard the name "Dr. Oxenbriggs," or simply "Doc Briggs." Even the sickest and weakest patients stood taller when they mentioned his name and recounted his visits.

"Came to my house long after dark to tend my grandmother," recounted one man.

"Never sleeps," said a toothless woman, drawing on a cigarette. "He met us at the hospital at 3 a.m."

The second year, Ash scanned the fairgrounds but never saw the doctor. Finally, in his third year, the legendary Dr. Nicholas "Briggs" Oxenbriggs cut a wide swath through the crowd as it parted before him. The great man paused long enough to speak to some of the throng of admirers and then strode to meet the group of returning interns and first years from Coastal Virginia Medical University.

Tall, sinewy, and muscular, moving with the comfortable grace of a lion who knew he was king, Dr. Oxenbriggs extended a lean hand that terminated in a broad smile surrounded by a rugged, tanned face filled with weathered charm.

One of the first years whispered to another, "Is that Harrison Ford?"

"Hello doctors," Doc Briggs boomed. "I am Dr. Nicholas Oxenbriggs, but everybody calls me Briggs. I am so thankful you are here. If you are not too tired after we close here tomorrow, and you have time, we can all meet for dinner. There's a great restaurant in downtown Big Stone Gap. 8 p.m. would be great, if you can make it."

Ash decided to go because he wanted to understand the affection everyone had for Dr. Oxenbriggs, and he would get a hearty, free meal. Thinking about his own future, he realized that having people admire you without question did bring certain benefits—not that he cared.

At the dinner, Dr. Oxenbriggs held court at the large, round dining table, asking questions, listening to the young medical students, learning about their ambitions and what drew them to medicine. Even the normally reticent Ash heard himself talking about his love for science and his passion for using verifiable data to help improve people's lives. Oxenbriggs listened with genuine interest, encouraging Ash to talk more about himself and intimating that there would be plenty of research opportunities here. "Should you choose to accept the offer," Briggs smiled broadly. "It's four years of the best people, the hardest work, and the worst heartache you will ever know, but it also means most of your student loans will be paid off."

By the end of the dinner, Ash was seriously considering the community health program at Lone Mountains Medical Center. Gazing at the smiling, confident Dr. Nicholas Oxenbriggs, Ash could easily see himself working alongside him, creating research and clinical trials among these desperate, but grateful people, hiking the mountains, fishing in the Clinch, and running along the beautiful trails. His student loans paid off in four short years.

Much later, Ash would recall this moment as his first step into Hell.

CHAPTER 3
Chronicling the Dead

Sometimes, Tierney Baynes wondered whether the dust that turned every surface of the newsroom a milky white had been in place for the century or more the paper, The Big Stone Gap Daily Star, had been in business. Hers was the only clean surface in the place and only because she hated dirt. Her grandfather jokingly referred to Tierney as "the person who put running legs on germs."

While most reporters show up with a notebook, cell phone, and a head full of cynical curiosity, Tierney arrived to her first day of work six months ago, armed with Windex, Lysol spray, and paper towels. Being toppled from her dream position as a government affairs and political reporter at a respected daily in Knoxville, Tennessee did not mean she had to work in filth. Although equally awarded and respected within the news industry, the Big Stone Gap Daily Star had always been just a tiny hometown paper. Therefore, it could not compare with the Knoxville Post & Courier, where her dreams had begun and abruptly ended.

Everyone said it. Newspapers were a dying form of

communications, but for Tierney and hundreds of other young hopefuls, this work was akin to life itself—pure journalism—what she had gone to school to do. Thirty years ago, this newsroom had been a nucleus of activity—filled with the constant clickity-clack of typewriters, the flurry of motion from reporters, pressmen, and three section editors, and the city desk, abuzz with the energy of news gathering. Now, the one room office dwindled to Editor and Publisher Will Hutton, one other full-time reporter, Emily Scott, a community page editor who doubled as advertising sales manager, a sports editor who came into the newsroom late Friday nights to write the game story, and the photo editor, Jeff Shapiro, who knew every back road shortcut in the entire region, and it was said he knew the names of every dog in the county.

Every few days, volunteer community writers carried in paper copies of their breezy columns, chock full of names of neighbors and friends with their comings and goings. Everybody in the area still loved reading their names in the paper, so this really was an important sales tool. People who had moved away decades ago still subscribed, scanning the pages for news about the mountain communities that were home to names familiar to them and long-lost family. The names of the communities, Crackers' Neck, Italy Bottom, Cadet, Pennington Gap, Keokee, and even Appalachia, translated to home for many people who had moved "off."

For this reason, Will Hutton rightfully claimed that the Daily Star was the local paper read "round the world."

"That's why accurately writing an obit and the obit profiles—getting the names, the praise, and the tone just right matters so much," Will had told Tierney when she protested her current assignment. "If you can get this right, there's hope for you as a journalist."

"Will, obits are for entry level, cub reporters," Tierney pleaded. "At least let me write features."

"I don't think anyone alive uses "cub reporters", "Will dismissed her. "You have to earn your way back. It's the only job I have for you."

So, here she sat, six months later, still writing obits and profiles about people after they died and thinking about who to blame for her present predicament. First, there was Will Hutton, who refused to let her do the work she was born to do. Then, there was that crooked cop, Eliot West. Yeah, he had put her here—he was most directly responsible. After all, he was the cocky Knoxville police detective that fed her false information, presented as tantalizing facts. She had convinced her editors in Knoxville that her source was reliable. They let her write the stories.

Perhaps she had miscalculated or added the numbers incorrectly. That was possible, but Tierney hadn't thought her math mistakes were worthy of a page 2 below-the-fold retraction, and nothing so dire as firing her. It was West who plied her with false information about drug busts and arrests. He was the cause of her dismissal. Now, they were both back here in their hometown, and the animosity they had nurtured through high school had blossomed into hate.

Tierney resolved not to let anger and righteous indignation take over. She double checked that her story actually was in the electronic filing system, known by the arcane term "the story bin." She made notes in preparation for the obit profile she had scheduled to conduct interviews for the next day. Then, she sneaked a look at her desk mate, Emily Scott, who was intensely typing and mumbling to herself.

Tierney cautiously secreted a worn reporter's notebook from a drawer in her desk. Glancing around the newsroom, she realized Will was not at his desk.

"Geeze, he's prowling around somewhere," Tierney whispered to herself. "I'd better hurry."

She flipped open the notebook and counted the names. Then, she counted several more from her computer screen that she quickly, but carefully numbered and dated, and then entered several names, dates of births and deaths, and addresses into her notebook. With a quick scan of the newsroom, she began to count the entries into the notebook. So absorbed was Tierney in the contents of the notebook, she did not see Will Hutton looming over her shoulder.

"29 in six months," Tierney whispered. "Damn, that's

out of whack. Something's wrong."

"What the hell are you doing, Baynes!" Will breathed in a loud whisper, which caused Tierney to bolt upward, nearly slamming him in the jaw with her head. He stepped back just in time, folded his arms, and stared disdainfully at Tierney.

Emily screeched, panted, and grabbed her heart. Pulling her turquoise rimmed glasses off her round face that was made up in brightly colored eye shadow and contrasting lipstick and framed by a cascade of purple curls, Emily spoke in her loudest little girl voice. Because of her diminutive stature, her creative style, and her innocent-sounding voice, people often didn't take Emily seriously, and that was just what she wanted. Beneath her warmth and seeming fragility, a calculating mind and a quick, analytical, and skeptical nature constantly assessed and planned how to get the information she needed without her source ever realizing her true goals. The only people who knew the real Emily Scott, besides her family of course, were now staring at her.

"Jesus, can you two please take your lovers' quarrel somewhere else? There are some of us who are trying to work and get out of here before midnight."

Releasing a tired sigh, Will shook his head. "Look, Em, I'm sorry. I know there are people who care deeply about facts and getting the story right." He avoided looking at Tierney, who tried to put her notebook out of sight and lighten the mood.

"Hey, Will Hutton," she protested. "I do care, and besides, you should not go around scaring us like that. Who would be around to write our obits if I die of fright?" She offered a sly smile.

"T. This is not a joke. I give you the damn lead story, and all you're interested in is another of your fake conspiracies," Will said. "I haven't seen the Medicaid scam story yet."

"I sent the Medicaid story to the rundown 20 minutes ago and then went out front to see if there were any paper obits," Tierney replied. "You know how I love writing those."

With a huff, Will pushed past Tierney toward his glass-enclosed office and plopped down at his cluttered desk, immediately punching a few keys on his laptop, where he began to read the story and mumble to himself. Tierney tried to discretely watch Will. Dark, black hair and dark skin that only drew more attention to his crystal blue eyes. Although Will was at least a decade or more older than Tierney, he would never look old to her, she was sure. He reminded her of that famous country singer or the late Clark Gable. They never aged and always took her breath away.

"A cool drink of water, that one," Tierney whispered.

"Tierney, not a good idea," Emily whispered.

"I know, Em. I know. You've been saving me from the wrong guy since grade school," Tierney said. "But he shore is purdy."

"He can also fire you," Emily said while typing.

Tierney forced herself to her work, counting the names again in her notebook, comparing that to the obituary list on her computer.

"T! Tierney!" Will's voice blared. "I got questions about your "confidential source" on this Medicaid story. Get in here."

"Will, you know my sources are solid," Tierney replied as she lumbered toward his office.

"Just because they may require less confirmation in the big city of Knoxville, doesn't mean you can get away with it here. We live in this town and face our readers every day—and besides—," Will had begun to lecture.

"Each. We face them each day, Will," Tierney corrected him. "Besides, I did bring down two corrupt police detectives while I was there."

"Yes," Will responded flatly. "Right down on the reputation of the paper and cost yourself your job in the process. Good going, and that won't happen here."

"Will, it wasn't my fault."

"Tierney, get a new song," Will cautioned. "That one's getting old."

CHAPTER 4

Little Boy Lost

Once upon a time, on any morning of the week, the crowds on either side of Wood Avenue in Big Stone Gap would have been so thick, locals described them as, "You can't cut them with a knife." But that was more than 40 years ago, when the mines were running full blast and provided good-paying union jobs that fueled the economy and underpinned the tax base. Towns like Big Stone Gap, Appalachia, Pennington Gap, and smaller communities like Dryden and Keokee thrived. Storefronts in Big Stone and Appalachia boasted everything one needed and more—the latest clothes, tools, sporting goods, and jewelry.

However, as the mines closed, the stores no longer showcased such abundance. One-by-one, the merchants shuttered their doors, leaving the once-vibrant towns lifeless and sad. Certainly, a few determined services carried on, and among them, the Mutual Drug Store seemed to thrive. Perhaps it was because so many people suffered so much more without the company doctors and union benefits and needed medicine. Two other services made the Mutual an exception. First, people could set up monthly payment plans, and second, the Mutual ran the best breakfast and lunch cafeteria anywhere. So, this became the nucleus of the community.

Dr. "Briggs" Oxenbriggs typically stopped by early each morning for an egg and toast sandwich and a large cup of the best coffee he'd ever tasted. He also took in the town gossip and gauged the community responses to the latest news. He especially listened to hear whether anyone held suspicions regarding the deaths of any of his patients. On any given day, most of the talk was when the coal industry would return and save them.

Briggs had grown accustomed to the adoring greetings as he made his way from the double glass door entrance around the perimeter of the cafeteria line toward the ancient register, where a smiling face greeted him. "Here you go, Doc," she said. "All ready for you."

"That is so sweet of you," he flashed a brilliant smile and held out a ten-dollar bill, which she waved off. "No, sir. You saved my Pappaw, and you ain't paying. Besides, it's only four dollars."

Oxenbriggs shook his head, pulled the girl's hand, and folded the money into it. He winked and slipped back toward the entrance, where along his way, people seated in the dark, brown, wooden booths reached out to touch him, each one speaking, smiling. Dr. Briggs had learned the art of engaging in polite, but evasive conversations, the type that allowed him to politely and quickly exit.

Stepping outside onto Wood Avenue, Briggs thought he had escaped the adoration and attention, only to be met by two retired miners, Jesse and Webb. Often, they still found work as handymen, so they frequented the Mutual to learn of any projects. Today, the pair bent over an open copy of the Big Stone Gap Daily Star. Briggs could see the headline on the front page as Jesse read.

"Wise County Doctor Charged with Millions on Medicaid and Medicare Fraud"

By Emily Scott and Tierney Baynes

On Thursday, the Federal Bureau of Investigation announced the arrest of Wise County physician on charges of filing more than five-million dollars in fraudulent charges. According to the indictment, Dr. Palmer E. Courtlandt allegedly billed Medicare for procedures that were never performed and for treatment on non-existent patients.

Dr. Briggs could not contain his curiosity. "What are you reading there, Jesse?"

"Oh, Doc Briggs," Jesse responded. "It's another in the Daily Star's investigations. Seems they've found more dirt since that girl Tierney Baynes came back than we've had in a hundred years."

"But this story is about that nice Dr. Courtlandt," Dr. Briggs said with surprise. "I know him, and he seems to care so much for his patients."

Webb shook his head. "He may well care very much for his patients, Doc Briggs, but he still has to eat and feed his family. Since the god damn mines closed, there aren't that many jobs with insurance. Who knows that better than you, Doc?"

"You may be right about that, Webb," Jesse folded the paper and stuck it beneath his armpit.

"What if a doctor or anybody took a little extra from the government? It's our tax dollars that feeds into them programs. Our tax dollars at work, I say. They shut down the mines, made a war on coal, and forced a bunch of hard-working people into poverty. Ain't no crime, and nobody got hurt, except a few fat cats."

Dr. Briggs started to walk away, but then the byline in the story caught his eyes. "Who is this reporter, Tierney Baynes?"

"Why, Doc Briggs," "Webb said. "You may not know her, but you treated her grandmother, Georgia Hood. She worked her way up from a secretary in the front office of the coal company to manager of the training for all the miners. She saved jobs and lives at a time when most women didn't have jobs."

"And she raised that girl after her mother died and her daddy run off," Jesse added.

Dr. Briggs took a step backwards. "I remember Mrs. Hood well. She was one of my favorite patients. What a wonderful person, but she passed peacefully. I was with her."

"Hey, Doc," Webb said, rubbing the small of his back. "Not to change the subject, but will you be at the community clinic this week? My back and legs are hurting so bad. I wonder if I've pulled something."

Doc Briggs hoped his sigh of relief went unnoticed. He was glad not to face any more comments about a patient that he watched slip from pain into eternal peace. Georgia Hood's drawn face had relaxed as she drew one long breath and lay perfectly still.

"Uh, of course, Webb," Briggs responded. Every Tuesday at 6 a.m. I will be there."

Glancing at Jesse, whose brown and missing teeth peeked out from beneath his long, gray, uneven moustache, Dr. Briggs thought for a minute before he spoke. These were proud, hard-working men, and he did not want to embarrass them. "And keep in mind that we have all the general health services there, like eye care, dentistry, and even physical therapy. It's all free, so I encourage you to make appointments in all the areas."

"Just like the RAM, only right here in Big Stone," Jesse said. "And we wouldn't have the clinic without you, Doc."

They didn't mention the Health Wagon, another of the altruistic services that exemplified the Appalachian natural spirit of caring for one another. Long before the Remote Area Medical weekend came to Wise County, The Health Wagon delivered care to people so poor they could barely afford to eat. Despite their poverty, most patients worked two or three jobs and made too much money to qualify for federal aid, but their jobs did not provide health insurance. The Health Wagon provided a remarkable service—delivery of mobile health, dental, and vision care to people who desperately needed help.

As Doc Briggs strode toward his old Ford F-150, Webb and Jesse watched in rank admiration.

Nudging Webb, Jesse said, "Ain't too many doctors who would drive an old truck like that."

Briggs turned, threw up a friendly wave and remembered the first day he met Webb. It had been at his inaugural Remote Area Medical Clinic, a decade ago.

At that time, the whispered suspicions were growing louder, like a constant riptide through the hallways of the small Ohio hospital where Briggs worked as chief of medical services. Experience told Nicholas Oxenbriggs the time to find a new position was at hand. There were too many questions coming at him.

He read about the three-day event in the New York Times, where it was described as "desperate people seeking one moment of health care" and "the result of a state's lack of action on health care." Dr. Briggs studied the photos of the pained and drawn faces. He ached to stop their hurting, to give each one of them eternal peace. He stood astonished at the massive need. Every spot on the fairground was covered with mobs of sick people. Many were old and already dying. He could help them. He could take away their pain.

After his first weekend, Nicholas Oxenbriggs knew what he had to do. So, he devised the familiar plan that had been so successful when he escaped Nevada in the 1990's and made a new life in Ohio. He would need three people in official positions to provide personal letters of reference, and Briggs had already charmed the human resources staff at the Ohio hospital. They would not hint at any negative concerns. Most of his patient deaths were not attributed to his license, and thanks to Briggs' unwavering love for his patients, none of their families suspected anything was amiss.

Further, the people in Wise County, Virginia needed him more. Luck and great timing seemed always to be on his side. Just as Briggs had made the decision to come to Big Stone Gap, one of the senior doctors announced his retirement, making room for the illustrious Nicholas Oxenbriggs to join the staff. He took it as a sign from Providence.

He moved into a rented house high above Big Stone Gap in Wallens Ridge Estates, a housing development on the hill that overlooked Big Stone Gap. The neighborhood grew after the opening of what the residents had hoped to be an economic driving force, the Wallens Ridge Prison. But from what Briggs could tell, it provided minimum wage jobs that would never replace the income from a $30 an hour coal mining job. That was one of the challenges here, finding suitable replacement work for people in an industry that had played out.

"But don't think too much about the past, old boy," Briggs told himself as he pulled away from Wood Avenue and headed toward Lone Mountain Hospital that morning. "Jesse and Webb are right. You are the best thing that has ever come to these old mountains."

Yes, "Briggs" Oxenbriggs had come a long way since the days of his childhood in Brockton, Massachusetts, the only child of a Frederik and Marina Oxenbriggs. Perhaps because his family kept him apart, never allowing him to "run the streets," the other children scorned the boy. He never had many friends, rarely played the neighborhood games or joined in the summer fun of the 1940's community. His father worked at one of the many shoe factories that surrounded the town and fueled its success. Although he was gone long hours, taking advantage of each hour of overtime available, when he was home, Frederik made his wife and son his world. His mother, tall and dark, adored her son and showered him with every advantage she could find. On the family's limited income, Marina wanted to show her son the world. There were monthly trips to the library in Boston, a summer trip once to the shore. Yet, Briggs felt all alone. He didn't fit in with the rhythm of the children, never quite mastered the art of "going along," and seemed more bewildered than angry when the boys in the neighborhood taunted him with, "Go home to your mother, Big Ox."

Briggs tried to hide his loneliness and frustration, realizing his parents would be unhappy if they knew, and he never wanted to hurt them. But as he reached the ripe old age of ten, Nick thought they knew, and he felt worse. That was the year that his mother became ill. But no one told the boy, so each time he saw his mother, Nicholas Briggs thought he had committed some terrible sin, and all he wanted to do was to make his mother smile. Yet, that was not to be.

She seemed tired all the time, taking to her chair by the window or her bed. She looked sad, and once, Briggs found her crying when he bounded in from school. She wiped away the tears and pushed through a smile. His father, too, lost his joy. There were hushed conversations when the parents thought Briggs was asleep, desperate glances and worried faces. But the darkest day of all began lush with green and sunlight, as only spring in Massachusetts can be. Eager to tell his mother about the new friend he made at school,

Briggs shoved the front screen door open with a bang. He didn't notice that the house stood in dark contrast to the sunlit afternoon. He had not seen his family car in the drive or the strange new vehicle pulled in behind it. When he didn't see his mother downstairs, Briggs bounded two by two up the stairs and crashed right into a strange man in a dark suit.

"Whoa!" Dr. Egglestein exclaimed. "I don't need two patients this afternoon."

Briggs froze, realizing in an instant that any news he had would never overcome the bad that this man represented.

"Mother? Where's my mother?" he stammered as the man rested a hand on Briggs' bony shoulder.

"She's in her room, and you must be Nicholas," the man said in a soft, consoling voice. "I am Doctor Egglestein."

Then, his father stepped slowly out of the bedroom over the doctor's shoulder and came to stand beside him. His face told Briggs that something more terrible than he had ever imagined had occurred.

"Nick, your mother is very ill," his father started.

Trying to jerk free of what he now realized was the doctor's tight grip on his shoulder, Briggs yelled and cried. The doctor pulled the boy close to him and let him cry.

"That's right, son," Dr. Egglestein said. "Cry and yell and get it out. Then, when you are ready, you can go in and see your mother."

That last comment gave Briggs the courage to stop crying. His father handed him a handkerchief, and the boy wiped away his tears. Summoning all his control, he nodded. The doctor released Briggs, and he followed his father into the bedroom, where his mother seemed to struggle to breathe. Each breath came harder than the last, and her once smooth face was drawn in pain. She forced a very tiny smile and tried to reach for her son. He fell onto the bed into her open arms.

"Mother, mother, what have I done?" Briggs tried not to cry. "I will do anything to make you better—anything. Please tell me."

Her words came one at a time, between gasps for air.

"Nicholas, you have been the angel who has kept me happy," she said. "You could never do anything wrong."

Frederik put his hand on his son's back, and still sobbing, the boy looked at his father.

"You didn't cause her to get sick," Frederik Oxenbriggs said. "You are the source of her—of our greatest joy. Now, no more of that. Your mother would like to hear about your news of school."

Reluctantly, Nicholas began to tell of his triumphant day, of making a new friend, but all the while watching his mother's face. He noticed she forced a smile between labored gasps. Briggs wanted so badly to stop her pain. He reached for her hand, and she weakly tried to pull him toward her. That's when he felt her rosary in her hand. She had never taken the piece of jewelry off her neck.

So, Briggs carefully slipped it from her weak grasp and into his own pocket. His mother took one last raspy breath and lay perfectly still. Her lifeless hand felt heavy in Briggs' grasp. He let her hand fall. After a moment, he felt his father's hand pulling him away, and he heard Dr. Egglestein's footsteps across the plank floor.

"Come Nicholas, she's with God and the angels," his father said softly.

Briggs watched as the doctor pushed in between the man now holding the boy and the bed with the lifeless body of the woman. Dr. Egglestein checked her pulse, raised a closed eyelid, then lovingly covered her over with the white and pink quilt she had made just after her marriage. He gestured for Frederik to step toward him and he guided him out the door. Once outside the bedroom, Dr. Egglestein gazed at the pair of lost souls before him. He wanted to say something comforting and hopeful, but there were no right words. One thing Dr. Egglestein had learned in his long career was to know when the heart of a family had died. So, he just patted Frederik's shoulder and mumbled that he would call the ambulance and make the "necessary arrangements." Then, he quietly tiptoed down the steps and out into the street.

Briggs wriggled free of his father's embrace and looked

back to the mound that had been his mother. At any moment, he expected her to toss back the quilt, rise, and come for him with a smile and outstretched arms. But that was never to be. She was at peace. Briggs heard the doctor and his father say that. He had watched her face as the pain and struggle drained away and were replaced by silent serenity. "That must be what peace looks like," Briggs thought. "No more pain."

"Father, I want to help other people find peace, like the doctor," Briggs stated flatly.

"It's a sad business, son, watching people pass," Frederik replied.

"I want to be a doctor," Briggs announced.

"That's an admirable profession, Nicholas, but it's very expensive to go to school. Not something I can afford on a shoemaker's wages. You best stick to the factory."

Pressing tighter on the rosary in his pocket, Briggs nodded. "At least I will always have mother with me," he said.

Frederik hugged his son and pulled the bedroom door closed. He did not shut out his son's determination to become a doctor. Over the next 18 years and with the help of the kind Dr. Egglestein and a few determined teachers, Briggs joined the U.S. Army, where he ultimately became a doctor in the early 1980's. He missed combat because he was too young to serve in Vietnam, and by the time the 1990s Gulf War erupted, Briggs was advancing his way up through the ranks of hospital and medical administration in Washington, D.C.

His father, long since retired, never remarried and maintained his home in Brockton even after the shoe factories had chased cheaper labor and higher profits to other countries. Briggs took all his leave time with his father, for he had learned long ago the fragility of life. He dreaded the day his father would pass like his mother did. But Briggs knew something now that he had not known as a small boy watching his mother writhe in pain. Briggs could stop the suffering. He knew it because he had learned to recognize which patients had the strength and physical ability to survive and which ones were just marking time. He had learned to help that group avoid the pain by helping them die.

Therefore, when the call came from a colleague in Boston that his father had been admitted to the hospital, Briggs knew it was time. He took an emergency leave, packed his medical bag, being certain to add the medication he had come to trust to help his patients avoid pain, and summoned the courage to execute the plan.

He found his father just as he expected, limp, struggling, and writhing in great pain, almost lost among the white, rumpled sheets. Briggs hardly recognized the strong, tall man he had known his entire life.

"It is time," Briggs told himself.

Carefully pulling a syringe from his jacket pocket, Briggs thrust its milky contents into the port on the IV tracing down into his father's vein. Briggs studied the wrinkled face before him as his father clinched his eyes closed in agony, took several forced, rasping gulps of air, then relaxed. No breath. No heartbeat. No pain. Peace. Forever. Briggs closed his father's eyes and calmly rang the bell.

"This is Dr. Oxenbriggs. I believe my father has just expired."

When the medical team rushed into the room, they found Briggs sobbing, hunched over his father's body. It would not be the first time, nor the last that the great doctor would play the role of the tragic, loving healer. It would not be the last time that a medical staff stood in awe of Briggs' compassion.

CHAPTER 5
Family Ties

Eliot West hated most parts of his job as the lowest ranking member of the Big Stone Gap Police Force. With an average of 15 sworn officers and five thousand citizens in the town proper, most never saw much action. Oh, there were the routine drug arrests, volatile, domestic brawls, and drunks. In the past few years, there had been joint sting operations with federal drug interdiction teams to break up illegal drug sales of the insidious opioid prescription drugs, a growing concern in almost every community in America.

But for Eliot West, those action-packed, intense investigations were the hearsay from fellow officers. For while they were out conducting what Eliot West deemed "actual police work," he was forced to patrol the main street, Wood Avenue, writing "Welcome to Big Stone Gap" parking tickets for those visitors who overstayed the limits on the parking meters.

Since returning to his hometown six months ago, this was all Chief Dove Black had allowed anyone to assign Eliot. What made everything worse was that all his fellow officers knew what happened in Knoxville. For his part, Eliot never regretted, never apologized, and never believed he was in the wrong.

What he had done was an economic necessity, and who got hurt? No one, no one at all. He had testified to that in his police commission hearing, and in the end, the internal governing body agreed. He received the lightest punishment possible. Six months suspended sentence without a permanent blot on his record. After that, his chief at the Knoxville Police Department fired him with the stipulation that he could not work in Tennessee again.

Eliot applied to police departments large and small across the country. Only one offered him a job—the last place he ever wanted to work—his hometown of Big Stone Gap. This was the place he had literally run from a dozen years ago, leaving behind his parents and the confining mountains that he thought he hated.

Even though one could drive to Knoxville in four hours or less, the cosmopolitan resources made it a new world. Eliot loved the pace, the constant movement, the arts, the nights, the busy days. He made new friends and met the woman he would marry.

Her name was Rhett Mackenzie, a raven-haired, vibrant beauty whose father was a retired firefighter in Knoxville. When Eliot first saw her, Rhett stood at the entrance door of the Knoxville Convention Center, directing people to seats at the annual city-wide fund-raiser for first responders. She had sass and a spark. After six months, they were married and moved into a small "starter" house in Fairmont on the city's north side.

For several years, their lives were happy, comfortable, and full of love. Rhett worked as an office manager in a doctor's office, and Eliot rose in the patrol ranks to detective. But good is just the other side of tragedy.

Eliot recalled the exact words Rhett said, "El, that fatigue I've had for months and that mole on my shoulder. Well, the doctor in my office told me today that it's cancer. I got the tests back today."

They held each other and cried. Built of the iron and coal of hearty mountain stock, Eliot knew no other way to face the fear than by looking directly into the fire pit. Skin cancer proved an unrelenting competitor. Each time they thought it had been conquered, the cells appeared elsewhere. Rhett fought back hard. But she could not work. Out-of-pocket expenses, extended chemotherapy sessions, and prescriptions drained the young couple's savings. Then, Eliot had a genius idea.

He had access to the police department evidence room. Alongside the active crimes, evidence from cases that had long since been adjudicated were stored there. What if he could take out some of the drugs, minor ones such as weed, and sell them to his street snitches? He could take in enough money to make up Rhett's salary in a very short time. No one would ever know, and no one would be hurt.

Eliot had a plan. There were no cameras in the far reaches of the evidence stores. So, he would choose one of his active cases for which there would be no questions asked when he pulled the evidence boxes. Then, he would watch the camera timings and slip to the rear to identify potential dead evidence. When he returned his case boxes, Eliot would lift the drugs and walk away. No one would ever know.

The plan worked perfectly. Eliot retrieved enough drugs, sold them, and paid for Rhett's prescriptions for one month. By that time, she was recovering. Another visit to the evidence room would cover the final round of medication. He easily stole the drugs, taking much more than the first time, sold them to his contact on the street, and again paid for his wife's life-saving medications. But the road to hell is paved with good intentions. The street contact was arrested by another officer during a drug bust. To avoid a life sentence for this, his third offense, the scoundrel exposed the source of his drugs. Eliot faced a long prison term, if convicted. However, his attorneys shrewdly opted for a service hearing before the commission. Although it could have recommended a criminal sentence, Eliot received the equivalent of a hard slap on the hand.

His wife recovered, then divorced him, saying she could never trust a man who put drugs back on the streets. Eliot had lost everything, but with a resolve borne of the mountains, he forged forward and took the only opportunity open to him: patrol officer on the Big Stone Gap police force, under the direction of the legendary and infamous Sheriff Dove Black.

That is how he found himself today, on Wood Avenue in the summer, writing "good will tickets." When he looked up from the ticket book, Eliot's day took a worse turn. Heading right for him, just past the card and gift shop, was the one person that Eliot had never wanted to see again—Tierney Baynes. She was the reason for his current situation. Tierney Baynes had gone to Knoxville for a job at the newspaper a few years after Eliot moved there. Although they had known each other throughout their years at Powell Valley High School, Tierney had escaped the mountains to attend college somewhere in Ohio. She returned to help care for her grandmother, who died too young. Once her grandfather had convinced Tierney that he would survive without her, she took the reporting job in Knoxville.

Eliot had been working in Knoxville nearly a dozen years when Tierney arrived. At first, they had been friendly. After all, they shared the same geographic history and the same culture. He often helped Tierney to understand how the big city police department worked, and she would give him as much information as possible when stories might affect him.

None of their information exchanges crossed the ethical lines or constituted anything illegal. Over a few weeks, the pair built a sort of trust. But it was not to last.

Tierney finally received an assignment that would end up on page 1A—a data-rich piece based on the annual crime statistics. In it, she compared the incidents to police staff assignment rates for each of the neighborhoods. The goal was to show that the most crime occurred in the areas with the lowest police presence. The numbers were all public record, but no one had put them together—overlaying the police duty assignments on the crime map. For the journalists, the tedious work would take time to conduct the analysis. Tierney and two other reporters worked for a week before they had the story.

Editors evaluated each segment, punching holes in the data and the conclusions and trying to determine whether the numbers told the accurate story. Everything except one neighborhood added up. But for that one, they needed another data point. How many police officers were on duty and in the area on the night of a huge bar fight that ended in gun fire and a death? It would take another week of research to find the answer, and when they did, Tierney and her compatriots were surprised that it appeared there were more officers than normal in the street that night.

Tierney took the numbers to Eliot for his insight and advice on how to reconcile them. With his help, the numbers made sense but didn't tell the same story as the other segments. After thinking about the outcome for a while and comparing the numbers, Tierney figured that making a slight adjustment in percentages would not change the outcome. But that one change required a similar adjustment across the board. Although Tierney's editors questioned the calculation, she was able to explain what had happened and cited her friend Detective Eliot West as her authoritative source.

"You cannot use his name," Tierney warned. "He is just my source."

But when the series of well-promoted articles exploded on the front page of the newspaper, followed by copycat stories on the local television stations, Eliot West was listed as a source and then quoted and requoted in all the news outlets. Tierney tried to find Eliot to explain. He refused to even see her. She begged in vain for her city editor to write a retraction.

For Eliot, that's when the real trouble began. His street snitch got greedy, demanding more drugs and threatening to embellish the amount of drugs he received. Eliot balked. Then, his snitch told a long string of lies with hints of truth to another detective, who was all too happy to tip off the one reporter he knew would never let the facts get in the way of a good story. As he suspected, Tierney was still gullible and inexperienced enough that she took the word of a police officer with little evaluation or question.

The editors at the Knoxville paper would not run the story until Tierney checked and rechecked the information. This included tracking down the street snitch, who changed his story again. This time, he claimed that Eliot blackmailed him into selling the drugs to avoid a charge of stealing them on his own. Though somewhat skeptical of the source for the story, the city editor decided to run Tierney's story with heavy attribution by the snitch, quoting both Eliot West and his fellow detective.

The day after the story broke, the police chief announced at a news conference that Eliot had been suspended until the investigation concluded. But everyone, especially Eliot, knew that the suspension really meant the end of his career. The only good was that Rhett was recovered and would survive the cancer. At least he had her, or so he thought. When he arrived at home on the day of his suspension, Rhett had cleaned out the house and left him. He had lost everything that mattered. The one thing he could do was to make a public statement that the numbers he had given Tierney were correct when he gave them to her.

Eliot's announcement ended Tierney's career as a legitimate journalist. No one would hire her. She would go home to Big Stone Gap and to her grandfather. Now, both Tierney and Eliot met on the same street in their hometown.

"Oh well, look what the cat drug in that the dog didn't

want," Eliot smirked.

"Glad to see you are doing important police work, West," Tierney goaded him.

"Baynes, isn't there some poor dog you've missed kicking today?" Eliot jeered.

Then, Emily Scott, who had been silent, spoke.

"Hello Eliot," she said in her lyrical, sweet voice. "I see you are putting out the "Welcome to Big Stone Gap" tickets. People from far off write or e-mail to tell us how much they love these."

"Emily, it's really good to see you."

"Eliot, I think ours is the only town that welcomes first time offenders," Emily said.

Eliot glared at Tierney. "Not a word from you, Baynes."

"Well, anything you do here will not be your first time," Tierney said.

"I have a whole row to finish here. Drama Days brings in a lot of people before the Trail starts," Eliot tipped his hat to Emily. "So, if you will excuse me." He pushed past Tierney toward the next car on the street.

"Do watch her, especially with confidential information. She doesn't know where to draw the line," Eliot said with insolence.

Emily shook her head. "Look, you two are home now. This is the place to start over, to renew, to build a new life."

They both glared at the smiling young woman with the

pink and blue hair, who wore a flouncy polka dot dress and clunky heels. She smiled broadly and with a push on Tierney's shoulder, directed her past Eliot toward the library on the upper end of town.

"We have to get to the library," Emily said cheerily. "I hope we see you later, Eliot."

When she thought Eliot no longer looked their way, Tierney chided Emily. "You of all people should not be nice to that snake. He dumped you two days before the senior prom, and you didn't even have anyone to walk with in the promenade. How can you defend him now!"

"It's in the past," Emily said.

"He tried to run me off I-40 after he got here. That's not in the past," Tierney said defiantly.

Emily shook her head. "Put your journalist's hat on, Tierney. It was dark, and you said yourself, you never actually saw a face, nor could you be certain what kind of vehicle it was. That's not evidence, and it doesn't sound like Eliot. Even you know that."

"Oh, Emily, you are still in love with that braggart," They were nearly at the library door. Tierney stopped and faced Emily. "My story cost him his career in Knoxville, and I'm sure he's not above revenge. So please be careful."

Emily waved her off. "You're living in the past, Tierney. Now, we have work to do. The databases here are free, and we need information to finish our story—the Medicaid fraud follow-up is due in two days."

Just as they started inside to the library, Emily stretched to her full, five-foot-five frame and peered back toward Eliot just in time to see the top of his head. He was running away from the cars—toward Bullitt Park and the police station. Something had happened. Once inside the library, Emily hurriedly plugged in her iPhone headphones and pulled up the police scanner app. Realizing that Emily had stopped, Tierney turned and walked back toward her.

"What's going on?" Tierney peppered her with questions. "Is there an accident? Somebody hurt? What happened?"

Emily waived her off, intent upon listening to the scanner chatter. "Tierney, please."

Routine communications. Officers checking on and off duty, announcing the status of patrols. Nothing unusual. Emily turned off the sound, pulled out her earphones, and thought for a moment. Whatever motivated Eliot to run at that moment had nothing to do with work. But something was wrong. She knew it.

"Hey, come out of your dream, Emily!" Tierney tapped Emily's shoulder urgently. "What the hell is going on?"

Emily shrugged, perplexed. "It turns out it must be nothing. I saw Eliot running just as we came into the library, but the scanner traffic is routine."

"Maybe he found that dog that needed kicking," Tierney smirked. "We have an hour, maybe less now. Come on."

The pair used the expensive databases available for the price of a library card. These same databases would cost their tiny newspaper an annual subscription well into the thousands of dollars, not something the owners could afford. Here, they could delve into personal information, including records of real estate exchanges, financial transactions, and legal matters.

Most of the public never realized what information was retained on virtually every detail of their lives. For the price of a subscription, most anyone could access this rich history. This is how reporters such as Emily and Tierney ferreted out information on the holdings of the doctor charged with Medicaid fraud. Here, they learned he owned property on Smith Mountain Lake, Virginia, an enclave of exclusive homes and lake front living. He also invested millions in some sort of off-shore financial investment firm, owned land in Barbados, and sent money overseas.

"He was planning to disappear," Tierney said.

"Well, it looks that way,"

Emily's comment brought Tierney back to reality. Emily was right. As much as Tierney wanted to write the story, there was not enough evidence to prove the doctor planned to leave the country, only that he had off-shore investments and land. She could almost hear Will Hutton.

"We need proof, documentation, Baynes," his crystal blue eyes piercing her. For Will, they would need airline tickets with the good doctor's name on them. When done correctly, the work of a journalist required meticulous attention to detail and writing only what you had the documentation to prove. Whether she wanted to admit it or not, Tierney knew that she preferred less work. Sometimes she found herself comfortable with the rumor mill and the assumptions that 21st century news-gathering relied upon for its "breaking news" stories. It meant you could be first, and that is what mattered most to her. She should have learned her lesson in Knoxville, but Tierney Baynes was stubborn.

Meanwhile, her arch nemesis, Eliot West, had more immediate concerns. What caused him to run was a phone call from his mother, Etta West. His father had been taken to Lone Mountain Medical Center. It was likely he had suffered another stroke.

By the time Eliot arrived, his father, Ira, had been moved to an observation room, which, in reality, was a rectangle cordoned off by white curtains in a long, skinny room, filled with two rows of identical rectangles. Eliot expected to find his mother hovering, but instead, Ira West held court as the center of attention in a ring of doctors in white coats. Standing nearest to Ira and taller than most everyone else was Dr. Oxenbriggs. He wore a broad smile, talking and gesturing to both Ira and the group. To the casual passer-by, this appeared to be a light-hearted and casual gathering, yet this could be life or death. Eliot's voice broke the reverie.

"Hello, Dr. Oxenbriggs? I thought my father came here because he was sick," Eliot said. "Looks like a celebration."

The group parted as Eliot made his way to stand beside his father's bed. Dr. Oxenbriggs stood on the other side, ringed by several medical residents. Eliot and his father shared the same crystal blue eyes, chiseled features, and open smiles. But Eliot was more muscular and not quite as tall as his father, whose years of working as a long-distance truck driver had taken their toll.

"I'm fine, son," Ira said cheerily. "I'm just here to help these young doctors learn. Right, Doc Briggs?"

A large, thin hand came to rest on Ira's shoulder. "That's right, Ira," Dr. Briggs smiled and gestured to the ring of interns. "I was just explaining to them that Mr. West had a slight stroke a few weeks ago and has been undergoing occupational and physical therapy, as well as being treated with some particular medications, to which he has favorably responded. But as you all know, stroke patterns are unpredictable. So, Mr. West is here with us again."

Eliot watched as the doctors nodded and took notes on iPads. He was sure most of them, if not all, had been recruited through the Remote Area Medical program. Eliot's mother had said many times that one of the many blessings of Dr. Oxenbriggs to this community was his ability to systematically attract these future healers and create the partnership with the University. After their training, these doctors would serve in remote communities here and in other places, their student loans forgiven and their talents and healing powers the gifts they would share with generations.

"Mr. West, you remember Dr. Ash McKay," Doc Briggs motioned as one of the residents stepped forward. "He will be assisting me with your care this time because I have a weekend conference. Now, where is Etta? I know she will want to hear everything first-hand."

"She's gone to park the car," Ira said. "You know her too well. That means we've been spending too much time in your good company."

As if on cue, a small powerhouse of a woman, with brown hair and matching brown saucer eyes, pushed back the curtain that divided Ira's observation section from the others. She was pretty and youthful, and many said she looked like a famous actress. Etta never paid real attention to compliments. Her focus was Ira and her son. Like a bee to honey, Etta charged between the gathering and made her way to Ira's side, nudging Eliot out a bit.

"There she is," Ira chuckled. "Now the doctor can tell us what's going on."

Etta lovingly smacked Ira's hand. "Ah, you and your jokes. Doc Briggs, please don't pay him no mind. Tell me."

"First, you tell me," Dr. Oxenbriggs gently chided. "You

went to Detroit against my orders, didn't you?"

"He had to see his brother—one last time, Doc Briggs," Etta admitted. "And to tell the truth, as you can see, it wore him out."

"You were not strong enough to make that trip, Ira," Dr. Briggs said in a stern voice. "You will take longer to recover this time."

"Recover?" Etta questioned. "He will recover, then. That's all that matters."

"But this time he will have to do what I say, understand?"

Etta nods furiously while Ira stares off, seemingly paying no attention to the people and conversation around him. Dr. Ash McKay notices that Ira is no longer engaged and speaks to him.

"Mr. West, I will be here over the weekend to take care of you," he said.

"Did you see that butterfly?" Ira West pointed to an empty space in the room. Everyone stopped talking and turned to look at him. "It was blue," Ira continued staring above toward the ceiling, but at nothing.

Dr. Oxenbriggs studied Ira, watching without intervening, as if he were a cat watching a cornered mouse. Only Dr. McKay acted. He shed a light into Ira's eyes, checked his pulse, and pulled out his stethoscope, placing the bright silver cylinder against Ira's chest and listening.

"I think we need some more tests. Would you agree, Dr.

Oxenbriggs?"

Only then did Oxenbriggs speak. Patting Ira on the shoulder and looking directly at Etta as if to reassure her, Oxenbriggs said, "I think you are on the right track, Dr. McKay. I approve your plan. Don't worry. We will get Ira better." With that, the great doctor and his entourage of admiring students whisked out of the observation area, leaving Ash McKay with the West family.

"Mrs. West," Dr. McKay asked, "has your husband had these kinds of incidents before?"

"Oh, Dr. McKay. He has been having these ever since we were here last," She wiped away a tear, and Eliot moved to hold his mother. "We've been doing everything that Doc Briggs said, well, except for the trip to Detroit. Do you think that caused this?"

"No, ma'am," Dr. McKay replied.

"Except for that drive to Detroit, which he insisted upon doing himself, I've made sure that my husband has followed Dr. Briggs' instructions," Etta said as she pulled a brown prescription pill bottle from her purse. "In fact, it's time for his pills now. Doc said not to miss even one dose."

Dr. McKay took the bottle and tried to hide his shock when he read the label. However, Eliot noticed the doctor's face.

"Well, Mrs. West, we need to hold on to these for now," Dr. McKay said slowly. "We need to run some tests without any medication in your husband's system."

Ash McKay hoped to get out of the room quickly enough to breathe and before Eliot West caught on and followed him. He was saved by Etta West, who called her son's name just as Ash opened the door and slipped out.

"Eliot," she said softly. "Would you do something for me, please? I am staying here with Daddy, and I wondered if you would sleep at our house?"

Etta watched her son for a moment, noticing that he looked haggard. She wanted to tell him to go home and sleep, but she knew her breath would be wasted. Etta hardly recalled Eliot breaking a smile since his return from Knoxville, and she wondered whether he would ever be able to live free of the hatred he carried so closely.

"Mama, I will when I finish my shift and come back by to check on you and Daddy."

Etta knew she had left a full cooked meal in the refrigerator, a large pitcher of fresh lemonade, and fresh sheets on the bed in Eliot's old room. She hoped he would find everything and succumb and she would find him sleeping soundly when she returned home. But there was no way to predict her son.

CHAPTER 6
Questions

Sometimes, in the quiet of twilight, Tierney thought she could hear the walls in the old, brick newsroom whispering secrets. She knew if they really could talk, she would be hearing the voices of history. She stopped typing for a moment to really listen. She imagined a time long ago when the newsroom at this hour crushed under the weight of frantic energy, with reporters, photographers, a couple of editors, typesetters, and designers pushing to meet the midnight deadline to "get the issue to bed."

Now, all were no more than vague thoughts in the mind of the very flawed reporter, Tierney Baynes, who wished she had been in the newsroom during its heyday in the 1940's and 1950's. That's when the war machine, starved for steel, pressed the need for coal. The "camps" overflowed with life. Each one boasted of several churches of differing denominations, sports leagues, garden clubs, a local store, a garage, and some had their own schools. For the Daily Star, this meant news items, sports stories, and calendar event listings.

Local residents volunteered to write breezy, chatty columns detailing events in their own communities, consisting of a litany of visits by out of town guests, births, birthdays, parties, and church socials. These seemingly innocuous "bits and bots," as one reader described them, proved ingenious revenue generators. For it seemed everyone wanted to read about their neighbors and even those who lived in other coal camps. These columns spurred many conversations around dinner tables throughout the mountains and well beyond, with people wondering who was related to whom, who had moved "off," and whether there were any scandals behind the printed activities. Given the popularity of "Community News," circulation grew as the coal industry, driven by the explosion in manufacturing, hired more and more men.

That lasted for several decades. However, by the early 1970's, the trickle of slowing manufacturing turned to a flood. In response, mining operations closed, shuttered forever. The owners could no longer support the system of corporate paternalism, as they had for decades, and the communities crumbled. No industry rushed in to replace the mighty 'King Coal." While the people waited for another half century for a reversal in the industry, the very foundations of their lives withered and dried up. Businesses reliant upon the good-paying jobs in mining could no longer sustain their existence, so they disappeared. Entire families moved north to Ohio and Detroit in search of jobs. Vibrant mining communities became memories covered in the grey cloud of coal dust.

By the time Tierney Baynes came to the venerable Big Stone Gap Daily Star, many of the coal camps had disappeared. Only a handful of the community columnists hung on to write what Tierney believed would one day be the obituaries for their beloved neighborhoods. She thought about what she would say if she had to write a profile of Exeter, Dryden, or Imboden—three communities that had somehow managed to survive. This thought reminded Tierney that she had a moment to review her list of suspicious deaths. She pulled a tattered reporter's notebook from her desk and began to review the names of the dead.

"What am I missing?" Tierney whispered to herself, examining the names again. She pulled a second notebook from her desk, opened it to a similar list, but this one was categorized by "Weird Statements by Family Members." When she cross-referenced the two lists, Tierney found the pattern.

"Holy magoly! It couldn't be," she exclaimed and urgently turned to her computer to search the Internet. "Loan Mountain Medical Center—physicians."

Tierney whispered to herself. "Virginia Board of Medicine." "Practitioner Look up." "Nicholas Oxenbriggs. Jesus H. Christ."

She didn't hear Emily's clicking heels as she flounced into the newsroom and plopped down at her desk with a tired exhale. However, Emily slowly leaned over so that she could see Tierney's computer screen.

"T. T! What is going on? Please tell me you aren't changing the direction of this story now," Emily demanded.

"Huh?" Tierney was startled.

"Tierney Baynes. We have put to bed the epilogue to last month's Medicaid fraud story. It's already in Will's bin." Emily chided. "Please tell me we don't have to start over."

"What are you talking about?" Tierney was genuinely confused.

"When you get all frantic like this, it usually means a change in direction. We don't need that now," Emily insisted.

"Remember the other day at the Mutual when Mrs. Turner was talking about her late husband? He died a few of weeks ago," Tierney pushed on, ignoring Emily.

"Yeah. Old people die. So, what?"

"Old! He was 63. She said he had been in good health then got sick suddenly. Then he kept getting worse," Tierney recounted. "Mrs. Turner said he was hallucinating, seeing things."

Emily yawned and settled on a bored stare. "I would like to go home tonight. Is there a point to this?"

"Emily, I heard the same story from three other people

about different patients. One was that woman I wrote about in the obit profile yesterday," Tierney's words rushed. "She was 65 and almost single-handedly kept up that old train depot in Josephine. Kept a community garden and taught outdoor skills to school kids. Her daughter told me she had not been sick until she cut her toe, got an infection. Next thing you know, she's in the hospital and dies. Hallucinations, too."

Emily shook her head. "And your point is? Old people dead. I don't need to inform you that is NOT news."

"Okay. The point is this," Tierney's rapid fire words spilled out. "It's the hallucinations and weird thoughts that perplex me. Why would three people suffering from different illnesses all have similar hallucinations and bad thoughts?"

"T—can you pay attention to the story in front of us—please?" Emily demanded.

"Em, this story is pretty much done," Tierney dismissed her concerns. "I'm always thinking about the next one."

"Then you'll have to find a good one because a 65-year-old dying is not news," Emily's frustration showed.

"You are a genius! That's it. They were all very active. Then went downhill with hallucinations. Death. Why?" Tierney asked excitedly.

Will Hutton could hear the voices of his two reporters as he walked from the pressroom in the back of the building to the newsroom. He heard Tierney's over the deafening clack of the press machine, and he was in no mood for one of her ever urgent, unfounded conspiracies. He tightened his customary scowl and emphatically cleared his throat as he tromped into the newsroom. Will was not surprised that Tierney prattled on without acknowledging his entrance. He knew that Emily heard him because she bounced back to her desk and purposefully began to stare at her slim reporter's notebook as if she expected to ferret out a winning lottery number.

"Tierney!" Will bellowed in his rich baritone. "That Medicaid story was last month. We all survived, and you didn't spend a night in jail. Good work." He nodded to Emily, who had looked up from her notebook expectantly. "Emily, as ever, solid journalism."

Tierney started to speak, but Will cut her off. "Tierney, I need those obits and that profile on the dearly departed Mrs. Snodgrass. Whatever conspiracy you're cooking up is over."

Tierney stood to face him, ever mindful that his piercing, blue eyes cut through to her very core. Had she not been so angry with him at the moment, Tierney would have melted. "Will Hutton, if this paper had not won so many national press awards under your leadership, I would not be working here," Tierney paused for a reaction, but there was none. So she continued. "When are you going to take me off obits and let me do more real reporting? Didn't I prove to you that I am a solid journalist? The TV 'journalists' are now sniffing around my Medicaid fraud story."

Taking a deep breath and closing his eyes, Will drew to his full, six-foot-plus height. Tierney could tell she struck a nerve and thought this may be the moment when he would finally relent. She could not have been more wrong.

"You are working here because I took a chance on an otherwise washed up reporter who made up statistics and could and would work cheap," Will spoke so softly and purposefully—the voice that none in the newsroom ever wanted directed at them. He continued. "A solid journalist meets deadlines and never questions her editor. I heard all that nonsense you're spreading to Emily and everyone in this newsroom. Enough!"

For the briefest moment, Tierney stared, speechless. Then she felt entitled and blustered on without realizing that with her every word, Will's temperature rose a few degrees. Tierney pressed on.

"Will, a solid journalist questions the editor all the time. Hell, she questions everything," Tierney pressed on.

Will folded his arms across his chest and sighed. "You look for too many problems where none exist. How could you of all people suspect a conspiracy at our hospital of all places! The place that takes in patients who they know can never pay. And your grandmother? Was she one of the victims? Didn't she die in her 60's unexpectedly?"

Now it was Tierney's turn to anger. That last remark about her grandmother hit too close to home. Tierney had done everything she knew of to save her beloved grandmother. They had been so close, so much alike. Her grandfather called them his "moon and star." He said his wife was the most beautiful creature on the planet until Tierney came along. His supercharged, little grand-daughter had helped the couple survive the death of their daughter. Although she worked full-time in the mine office, Tierney's grandmother volunteered at school, attended all of Tierney's sporting events, and stayed up late just to talk. Her grandfather and grandmother became Tierney's greatest fans. When her grandmother had a heart attack, Tierney and her grandfather never left her side, except for that last day at the hospital. She ordered the pair to take a walk in the fresh mountain air. When they returned, Doc Briggs stood there by the bed, which contained the lifeless body of the woman who had been the luminous moon in their lives. Doc Briggs nearly cried as he shook his head in defeat. Will Hutton should have known better.

"Leave my personal life out of this," Tierney fought back tears. "My grandmother's death at such a young age, and when she was in perfect health the month before, has nothing to do with what I've uncovered, and this is not a personal crusade."

"Tierney, Tierney. Will you listen to yourself?" Will almost pleaded. "Old people and other people die. Sudden death, car crashes—even healthy women in their prime get cancer and die. It's not always a conspiracy."

It was only then that Tierney realized what she had done, blundering on the way she did. Will's wife had died three years earlier, the victim of a deadly form of melanoma that acted all-too-quickly. Even the best doctors in Knoxville could not save her. So, Will had brought his bride of 20 years home to the peace and mountains of Big Stone Gap, where she died in her sleep one brilliant, fall morning. He loved her dearly and could think now only of his children and his work. His two girls were nearly teenagers now, and they thought they didn't need their father. His mother and his wife's mother had stepped in to help him. Fortunately, they got along and agreed on how best to raise the girls. This allowed Will to concentrate on his work, not having to think of the emptiness of his home.

"Will, your wife. I am so, so sorry," Tierney stretched her hand to touch his arm, but he slid away from her.

"I took a chance on you, and in a small community, it's not easy to defend my decision," Will said flatly. "We win awards here because we do solid work, not because what we do is sensational. Get back to work."

Will marched off to his desk. Tierney and Emily watched him go with a mixture of pain and love, but Tierney was not at all remorseful for anything she had said or done.

CHAPTER 7

Dead Ends

Something about the way that young medical resident, Ash McKay, acted made Eliot West suspicious. He was sure something was wrong, and that doctor knew a great deal more than he was letting on. Perhaps his father was worse off than they were saying. Perhaps it was something in the treatment plan or the medicines. Doctor McKay did seem to concentrate on that bottle of pills his mother held so tightly. That seemed to be the place to start, Eliot believed. He would have to sneak a look at that bottle or chart when his mother wasn't looking. Trouble was, Etta West never took her eyes off anything. But with his dad still in the hospital, perhaps Eliot could get his hands on the chart when Etta stepped out for a minute. Perhaps he could get her to go for a walk if he promised to sit with his dad. Convincing Etta would not be easy.

Eliot stopped by his dad's room just before his shift, which began at 3 p.m. As expected, Ira slept peacefully, and Etta sat straight up, watching him. She would not allow herself to recline, rest her eyes, or even take her feet off the floor. Eliot knew she must be exhausted and worried, but he also knew she would keep smiling through it all.

"Mama, how is he?" Eliot whispered.

Etta touched her son's arm and looked at him with those saucer brown eyes he loved so much. She shook her head. Eliot tried not to show his concern.

"He's still seeing things and hollering," Etta whispered. "I just don't know. I wish Doc Briggs would get back."

"Mama, listen, it's a beautiful afternoon, and the air is fresh. Why don't you go take a walk?" Eliot implored. "I will stay with Daddy." He watched her face for any sign that she would agree. He waited, smiling at her and nodding in encouragement.

Etta studied her son's face, then looked at her sleeping husband. Surely, he would be alright for a few minutes, and the sun would feel good. She would go, but just for a few minutes. She nodded, and Eliot helped her to her feet. Etta silently tiptoed out of the room, offering one last look at the two men she loved most in the world as she silently closed the door behind her.

Eliot moved quickly as soon as his mother was out of sight. Unfortunately, she had taken her purse with her, so he would have to rely on the medical chart hanging on the foot of the bed. Luckily, Lone Mountain had not moved to computerized charting yet, as many larger facilities had done. Much of the information was incomprehensible, but he could read the list of medications. He pulled out his phone, moved as far as possible from his father's bed, and clicked as many photos as possible. He flipped through the pages and took a couple more photos even though he had no idea what they meant; the information may be important later. Just as he was about to replace the chart, the door flung open, and Ash McKay walked in. He stopped short when he saw Eliot with the chart.

"Hello Mr. West," Dr. McKay whispered. "Where's your mother?"

Eliot tried to slip the chart back on the hook, but it clattered to the floor, disturbing Ira West.

"Hey, hey!" Ira called out. "What's happening here?"

Eliot and Dr. McKay reached Ira's bedside at the same moment. McKay raised Ira to a sitting position and softly said his name, while looking intently as Ira's face. "Mr. West, it's Dr. McKay and Eliot. Did you have a good nap?"

"Dad, you're looking good," Eliot lied. His father would know right away, but something was wrong with Ira West's keen mind. He just smiled toward Eliot and nodded. Eliot looked to Dr. McKay for an explanation, but McKay gave up nothing. He pulled a pencil sized light from his breast pocket, flicked on the bright light, and pointed it toward Ira.

"Mr. West," Dr. McKay said. "I'm just going to check your reflexes, take a look at your eyes. This will be bright for a moment."

Ira squinted as the light pierced his eyes, but said nothing. Eliot noticed that the usual mischievous glint had vanished from his father's eyes. Something was really wrong, and Eliot realized that Dr. McKay had the same thoughts. He turned off the pencil light, placed it back into his lab coat pocket, and then rubbed his forehead as if struggling to collect his thoughts to come up with an answer for Ira West's deteriorating condition. He performed a mental checklist.

Over the course of the last five days, Ira West had undergone occupational therapy sessions to improve his swallowing and motor skills. He had conducted all the necessary scans to ensure there were no additional blockages, and most importantly, Dr. McKay had stopped the Haldol pills that had wreaked havoc with Ira's mental state and overall physical well-being. That drug, meant for schizophrenics, should never have been prescribed for Ira West. His last dose should have been five days ago, and by now, Ira should be returning to a predominantly normal state. But he was not.

Walking to the foot of the bed and picking up Ira's chart, Dr. McKay carefully reviewed all the orders. He did not see anything to indicate the drug had been ordered again. Yet, Ira's vital signs had sharp changes. That was a certain indication of some external influence. McKay was upset with the nursing staff. They should have notified him. He wrote furiously, adding some new blood screens and additional brain scans. He was sure some solid science would tell him whatever was happening to Ira West. What he couldn't imagine at that moment was that Ira West's deterioration was caused more by love and blind faith.

Etta West returned to find Ira sitting up, flanked by her son at Ira's right and Dr. McKay at the foot of the bed.

"Well, I am so glad you are awake, Ira," Etta said. "You must be hungry. Doctor, could we get some food for Mr. West, please?"

Upon the sight of Etta, Ira managed a weak smile. "I could eat, "he said slightly above a whisper.

Etta marched right to her husband and kissed him on the head. She looked at Eliot. "Can you stay and eat or–"

"I need to get to work, Mama. I can later," Eliot said. He, too, was trying to determine what was making his father worse, and he was anxious to get to a place away from the hospital where he could review the photos of his father's records to see if there was a clue he could understand. Eliot had seen enough in his career to know that the good doctor, Ash McKay, was hiding something as well.

With a quick hug to his mother and a wave to his father, Eliot left the room. As soon as he was safely in the hallway, he pulled up the photos on his phone and scrolled until he found the one with the list of medications. He didn't know any of them immediately, but would look them up as soon as he got to a computer. He also planned to talk to Dr. McKay. Something was not right, and Eliot sensed the young resident knew what it was.

Meanwhile, Dr. Ash McKay was working on his own investigation. Even though he had no proof, Ash was certain that Mr. West was somehow taking Haldol. Considering how much weaker Ira had become in less than a week, there was no time to wait. So Ash McKay did something he never did. He trusted his instincts.

"Mrs. West," Dr. McKay tried to control his voice. He needed to win her trust. "I've just finished a routine examination, and your husband is not bouncing back as quickly as we had hoped. I am hoping you can help me."

Etta looked shocked and pale. "Uh, well, Dr. McKay, you know I will do all that I can, but shouldn't we wait for Dr. Briggs to return to make any changes?"

McKay knew he had to get the answer precisely right, or Etta West would raise a ruckus with the nurses' station until someone called Oxenbriggs. He also knew she did not trust anything he had said so far. His only advantage was that Oxenbriggs had left him in charge, and he could use that to gain Mrs. West's trust.

"Mrs. West, would you agree that if Dr. Briggs thought that getting Ira better could wait until he returned, he would have said that? Instead, he left me in charge and trusted me to do the right thing. We both want Ira well,"

Ash watched her face change from stone-cold resistance to acquiescence. He pressed forward with something that felt alien to him—a hunch.

"You are still giving Ira those pills?"

"Well, yes," Mrs. West stated emphatically. "After YOU took my bottle, I went to Kingsport to get a refill. The Mutual said they didn't have any in stock."

"Oh, did you get the generic?"

She nodded. He seized the opportunity.

"They have different bonding agents. Why don't you let me test them down in the lab to be sure they will be effective?" Ash held out his hand and waited. Etta reluctantly reached down into her pants pocket and slowly pulled out the brown bottle.

She looked at it and then at Dr. McKay who was nodding and smiling confidently, patiently. Etta slowly placed the bottle into his open hand. Ash clasped his free hand over hers, consoling. To Ash's astonishment, Etta stood and hugged him.

After a moment, she released him and wiped a tear from her eyes.

"I am trusting you to take care of the most important human being on the planet, Dr. McKay," Etta swallowed and studied his face.

"Don't worry, Mrs. West. We have the same goal. Now, let me get these pills to the lab," he said, walking toward the door. "And please, let us give Ira the medication he needs from the hospital pharmacy. No more bringing medication from the outside."

Ash slid out of the hospital room door and almost collided with Eliot West, who was leaning against the hallway wall, studying something on his phone. Both men hurriedly apologized, and then they recognized one another. Eliot spoke first.

"Dr. McKay, I need to ask you about my dad's medication. Something is not right, and you know it."

He waited.

Dr. McKay chose his words carefully. "We are going to get to the cause of your father's recurrent spells and get him well."

Eliot didn't buy the answer, and McKay knew it. Eliot stared at the doctor, who finally spoke, and this time, Eliot knew the words were closer to the truth.

"Mr. West, your father is having a reaction to one of his medications. I think it is the one your mother is bringing into the hospital. I just convinced her to give me the bottle she got in Kingsport. I will know more after some tests. Meanwhile, please help me by ensuring that she doesn't give him any more of those pills. Eliot believed McKay, but sensed there was more. So, he gave the doctor his best "tell me more" look in dead silence. Ash squirmed and began to talk, his words tumbling over one another.

"Mr. West. We will do everything we can to get your father well, but I need your help with your mother," McKay couldn't stop for once. His formal control had abated. "She is bringing in this medication, and your father no longer needs it at all—if ever he did."

"Wait, what do you mean, Dr. McKay?"

Ash realized he had said too much, especially to a police officer. He tried to recover and struggled to regain his normally placid expression. "I mean that your father doesn't need the medication—Haldol. I've taken the last bottle that I know exists from your mother without alarming her. Please help me by letting me know if she brings in more of it. That's all." Ash looked at his watch. "Mr. West, I need to get these tests started for your father. Sorry, but I need to go."

Eliot could not argue, so he stepped aside to let the harried doctor pass by. He resolved that he would find out what was really going on himself.

Out of the watchful sight of Eliot West, Dr. Ash McKay picked up charts from the nurses' station and headed off to what he knew was an empty hall in the hospital. It had been under renovations, so the only things Ash expected to find were empty patient rooms and construction equipment. For the most part, he was not surprised. He had seen Dr. Oxenbriggs come this way a few times and thought perhaps the doctor had found a quiet place to decompress.

To his surprise, McKay found a desk with a working lamp and a chair in one of the treatment rooms. This must be where Briggs came to rest. So, McKay sat down at the desk and spread the charts around him. He didn't have much time, so he hurriedly looked through them for a common thread, starting with medications prescribed. And he found it in the first five charts.

"That son of a bitch!" McKay slammed his fist on top of the charts. He quickly gathered them and headed back to the nurses' station. Once in the hallway, McKay slowed to a commanding pace, smiled at the staff he passed, then calmly dropped the charts onto an open desk space and began to replace them one at a time into their respective slots.

"Let me help you, doctor," said one of the nurses, reaching to take one of the charts from the desk and sliding it into its slot.

Ash feared the nurse would ask more questions, but he did not. Instead, he refiled the remaining charts, and as silently as he appeared, the nurse disappeared down a hallway. Ash stood for a moment, wondering what he should do next. He now had more than suspicions, but no real proof. If he tried to investigate further, he risked his hard-won career. Dr. Oxenbriggs was clever, capable, and certainly would know.

What Ash needed was someone outside the system, someone who knew how to ask the right questions, gather evidence, and do so discreetly. But he had no one he could trust. "Or," he thought, "Do I?"

Moving to a quiet corner, he dialed the number for Eliot West. "We need to meet, away from the hospital, to talk about your dad," McKay said.

Somehow, the call didn't surprise Eliot. He knew something was truly wrong. He agreed to meet the resident that night near The Mutual Drug Store. It would be closed by midnight, when Eliot's shift ended.

These days, not too many people ventured out at night in downtown Big Stone Gap. Times had long passed since three shifts at the mines meant nearly round-the-clock people trafficking in and out of one late night diner or another. But now, Wood Avenue, cast in shadows, remained silent. In an effort not to raise suspicion, Eliot drove away from the police station as if he were heading home, then doubled back. He parked a few blocks away and walked up from the back, waiting out of the glow of the street light.

Ash McKay may as well have held a parade down Wood Avenue to announce his arrival. He pulled his Prius right into the parking space in front of the Mutual, and its lights temporarily blinded Eliot. He stepped back as far as he could into the darkness, but feared that someone had already seen the flashy hybrid car. He did his best to make a scan, but saw nothing.

Ash nervously looked around and nipped straight over to Eliot.

"Okay, what's going on, Doc?" Eliot paced in the darkness, and the questions and answers came in rapid fire.

"Look, I'm a final year resident," Ash sputtered. "But I've been in medical training almost eight years now. My career is gone if I'm wrong."

"You brought me here to tell me about your credentials?" Eliot's frustration bubbled.

Ash had to get it all out in his own way. "I want you to be able to trust what I'm about to tell you. I have no motive except the wellbeing of my patients. And what I am about to say could destroy my career."

Eliot warned Ash. "Doc. I am accustomed to people lying, cheating, stealing, and telling me they are innocent. You cannot fool me or shock me. But you said patients?"

"Are you familiar with the medications that have been prescribed for your father?" For the first time, Ash McKay stared at Eliot.

That caught Eliot off guard. "Why?" He demanded.

For once, Ash answered the question he was asked. "There is one that has serious side effects if prescribed for the wrong reasons. It was given to your father."

"You brought me up here to tell me that you gave my father the wrong medication?" There was a mixture of confusion and frustration in Eliot's voice.

"When I realized he was taking that medicine that day in the ER I took him off it." Ash explained. "I even had your mother give me the bottle she kept in her purse—but she still has another. I'm sure of it."

"My mother is responsible?" Eliot fought hard to control his rage.

"Mr. West. I know you are a police officer, skilled in interviewing, and that you have no reason to trust me. But please let me explain," Ash was pleading for understanding, but he could tell that Eliot had no patience.

"You are talking about my family," Eliot demanded.

Ash could see that Eliot looked more like an exasperated patient. It was time to make his point. "Let's agree on one thing. We both want what's best for your father."

"Done. Now cut to the chase."

"This is hard. It's almost unbelievable. But here goes. That drug is called Haldol." Ash felt the words rushing out of him, without control and without the usual consideration he gave each word. "It's a well-established treatment for schizophrenia. In simplest terms it helps settle the mind. But in normal people, Haldol, in any form, can cause hallucinations, violent outbursts, strokes, and even death if given in sustained doses. Your father was prescribed that drug. I had to do my research. I am, first of all, a scientist. But now, I've been able to review your dad's entire history. He's not schizophrenic."

"All you had to do was ask me," Eliot growled.

"He doesn't need that medication at all." Ash looked for any sign of surprise or shock in Eliot's face, but all he could see in the shadows was sullen impatience.

"Can we come to the point?" Eliot resisted the urge to shake the words out of the young doctor.

Ash took a breath. "What I am about to say is shocking, and I must ask you to keep my name out of it. But, well, it's Dr. Briggs Oxenbriggs. He's writing the prescriptions."

"Prescriptions? More than my dad? Why would you say such a thing about a doctor that many consider a god?" Eliot didn't believe what he was hearing, but the investigator in him told him to calm down, to listen with cold intent. "I say this because, because it's true. Someone has to stop him."

Eliot began to pace slowly in the darkness. "Is my father safe?"

"If he doesn't go see Dr. Oxenbriggs again." McKay circled to stand in front of West, who came to a stop. The two men faced each other in silence for a moment.

"Why are you saying Oxenbriggs the man who's done more for this community than anybody—is deliberately doing this?" Eliot's anger overtook him. He pushed forward, forcing Ash to stumble backwards. He recovered his balance and came again to face Eliot.

"Deliberately? I'm not sure. But you can find out, and you can keep my name out of it."

"Wait a damn minute? Me? What makes you think I can do anything? And what if you're the one doing this? Good play to take suspicion off Doc Briggs." This time, Eliot planted himself to face Ash McKay.

McKay took a step toward Eliot and raised his arms in a questioning gesture. "Why would I tell you all this if I were the person doing this? You're a police officer. I've told you something suspicious. Now, you can investigate."

Eliot leaned into Ash's face a little too closely. "Look, I'm sure of one thing. I want my father to be safe. I'm not sure about anything you're telling me. Hell, you could be poisoning my dad for all I know."

McKay didn't back down. "I am risking my entire career by coming to you with this. Dr. Oxenbriggs supervises my residency. If he finds out I am talking to you, I'll never work as a doctor. So, I have plenty to lose."

"He has a lot of patients and respect in this town. That could all be yours," Eliot taunted McKay as if he were a suspect.

This gave McKay a moment to collect his thoughts. "Then try this. Oxenbriggs signs off on my treatment plans not the other way around." He watched for a reaction from Eliot.

Eliot stepped backwards and looked at the ground. He recalled reading his father's medical chart, where most of the signatures were indeed Oxenbriggs'. He now believed McKay and wanted to keep him talking. He thought perhaps, he could seem to be helpful.

"All right. I am not promising I can do anything. But what will you do?" Eliot questioned.

Ash McKay stepped back and paced in the shadows. Eliot realized he was considering options. "Try this. Dr. Oxenbriggs is going to be at the medical conference in Louisville. I will treat your father directly for the next few days. I'll discharge your dad before Briggs returns," McKay nodded. "He will be stable. Then, you need to get him to go to Kingsport or Knoxville somewhere with bigger hospitals, plenty of doctors. Just see anybody in that city. Just don't see Oxenbriggs. Another round of this drug could be fatal." McKay emphasized his statement by standing still, staring at Eliot, waiting for a response.

Eliot realized he would have to take action and immediately understood there was a major obstacle. "The problem is my mother. She thinks Oxenbriggs is a god."

A small smile broke across McKay's face. "I understand that one. I've met your mother. But, you may be able to save more than one life."

The statement caught Eliot off guard. "What! What the hell do you mean?"

McKay had already started back toward his car. "You just take care of your father," he warned Eliot.

CHAPTER 8
Mementos

Over the decades, the Big Stone Daily Star newsroom had seen its share of luminaries and important people. Famous stars of country and bluegrass music, writers, painters, and artists had all stepped across the threshold of this venerable newspaper, hoping for a front-page story. That would have solidified their position in their chosen fields. Others were community leaders or supporters of causes who wanted a front-page story, realizing the importance of this tiny, mountain paper.

Although her family was prominent for their community involvement throughout Wise County, Barbara Patton did not want to be in the newsroom on this day at all. In fact, she wanted to be anywhere else. But here she sat, across the ancient desk from a young reporter who feigned interest in her story. However, Barbara did want this story publicized for one reason. She wanted to find her mother's heirloom, ruby broach. In her mid-fifties, with naturally brown, short-cropped hair and deep-set, green eyes, Barbara sat straight and poised, offering Tierney a serene smile. She pulled her cashmere jacket tighter around her shoulders and brushed the sharply pleated legs of her soft, wool pants while she waited for the reporter to find a pen among the stacks of rubble on her desk. Finally, the reporter held a pen in the air.

"Got it!" Tierney exclaimed.

Barbara nodded and smiled again.

Tierney's words streamed out. "Mrs. Patton, I really appreciate your coming to the paper for this interview. I would have been happy to come to your house. I routinely do that for a profile of someone so special. So, tell me about your mother, Elizabeth Langford."

At first, Barbara tried to control her words and her emotion. She did not cry in front of others. It simply was not done. The question was not what she expected. "Ms. Baynes, my mother was bright, lively, and energetic. She started trail runs here, you know? In fact, she was on a trial run for a new race when she started having chest pains," Barbara paused and swallowed so that she would not sob. "Even then, she told the group with her that she was fine. Didn't want to worry them. She kept smiling. She drank the light and air when she entered a room."

Barbara Patton struggled to retain her composure by changing the subject. "Tell me, Ms. Baynes. How did you come to have such a lovely first name? I'm sure there's a story there."

The reversal of roles flustered Tierney, who had her next question ready. "Oh, it's not much of a story. My late mother enjoyed the film star Jean Tierney for a lot of reasons. She liked her determination and her unrelenting pursuit of her career. So, when I came along Tierney I became," She wriggled and displayed what Barbara would call a "little girl before finishing school" smile. Barbara would calm down, despite her grief. That would be in her best interest. Just keep the red-haired waif talking.

"Are you much like your namesake?" Barbara asked softly.

Tierney relaxed. "My grandfather says I'm stubborn and determined. But those are the words of a loving grandfather," Then, Tierney changed the subject. "Anyway, do you feel like talking about what happened, Mrs. Patton?"

"Of course, my dear," Barbara said in her soft, comforting tone. "Three weeks ago, she went into the hospital with chest pains. The doctors in the ER said it was most likely a mild heart attack. But they wanted the cardiologist from Kingsport to review her results. He would be in the next day. Then, Dr. Oxenbriggs came in decided she needed to be admitted right then. He took over." Barbara paused, remembering how Briggs swept in, and the sea of medical professionals all fell back, as if they were watching Jesus Himself enter the room.

Tierney feared the pause, so she pressed Mrs. Patton for more information. "And what happened next?"

"After a few days, things took a bad turn. My mother started hallucinating not recognizing any of us. We called the cardiologist, and he said, in so many words, that Dr. Oxenbriggs had told him there was no need to come," Barbara said.

This time, Barbara could not hide her pain, which was reflected in the tear that rolled out of her eye. Tierney gave her a moment to collect her emotions.

"Wait. I don't understand. Are you saying that Dr. Oxenbriggs cancelled the cardiologist for a woman who may have had a heart attack?"

Barbara shook her head. "We're not sure what happened."

Now it was Tierney's turn to be perplexed. "So, did your mother have another heart attack, or what happened?"

Barbara sighed deeply. "We don't know. Over the course of five days, she lost her mind—and please don't print that part or this next one. My mother was so strong, so in control. But, she started seeing things. Then, she didn't recognize us at all. It was such a crazy, sudden thing," Barbara paused for a moment, studying Tierney's face as she furiously scribbled in her slim reporter's notebook.

Tierney had to be careful with the next question because people in the mountains were not fond of autopsies. They viewed it as a violation of the body. So, Tierney approached the question delicately.

"Mrs. Patton, I have to ask you something hard," Tierney

had stopped writing and looked softly at the refined lady facing her. "Did you have an autopsy?"

The momentary pause allowed Barbara to remember why she agreed to this interview in the first place, and so she ignored the dreaded autopsy question. She wanted to talk about her mother's ruby broach. "The worst part—it wasn't until after we got through the funeral that we realized Mother's ruby broach that she wore all the time was missing."

Tierney had all the answer she was going to get about an autopsy, so she shoved her pen over her ear and stared lovingly at Barbara. She wanted the older woman to believe she cared, so for once, Tierney chose her next words carefully. "How sad. I am so sorry because it was a memento of your mother. Did you ask at the hospital?"

Barbara didn't answer the question directly, something Tierney had grown accustomed to with story subjects. They had their own way of sharing information, and if she learned nothing else, Tierney had learned how to get people to open up, she thought. After a moment, as Tierney expected, Mrs. Patton continued.

"The day my mother died, the young resident, Dr. McKay, was with her. He said she passed peacefully, but there was nothing he could do. He was practically crying. I didn't have the presence of mind to ask about her things at that moment," Barbara said with a long sigh.

"Wait! McKay!" Tierney practically jumped from her desk. "Not Dr. Oxenbriggs?"

Barbara Patton shook her head and offered Tierney a perplexed look. She said that until just the day before her mother passed away, Doctor Oxenbriggs had been on duty, in and out of the room. But he had been called away to Russell County or somewhere, and that was the day Mrs. Elizabeth Langford had chosen to exit the world. The nurses found her still and peaceful on their routine rounds.

"That young resident, Dr. McKay, talked to us," Mrs. Patton said softly. "He seemed so sad, and it was all so sudden that none of us realized the broach was missing."

She added something that made Tierney stop writing.

"I wish Dr. Briggs had been there. He was genuinely sad when he heard she had passed, saying he loved my mother and she was his favorite patient."

Mrs. Patton then explained they had asked about her mother's things the day before the funeral, when they looked for the antique, multi-leaf broach with its varied, colored leaves and the ruby in the center. Without much time, the family proceeded with the funeral without the broach.

"It was very emotional," Mrs. Patton said. "But we had no choice. We asked the hospital staff, but no one recalled seeing the broach on the day my mother passed. Dr. McKay insisted she was not wearing the broach when he, uh, well, m-m-h, when he was in the room on that last day."

Mrs. Patton said her husband and sister insisted they file a formal police report, which she had done last week, but so far, no one had offered any information. Mrs. Patton said she planned to follow up with the sheriff's office that day, after the interview.

My mother was 85, but very, very active. She taught an active lifestyle class at the community center and led senior adult walks at Bullitt Park. She volunteered at the June Tolliver House, and, well, I'm still in disbelief," Barbara Patton shook her head and stood. "Thank you, Ms. Baynes."

Tierney watched Mrs. Patton walk away, then pulled another notebook from her desk and began to write. She carefully counted numbers and then looked around the newsroom for Will. She saw him at his desk. For a moment, Tierney allowed herself to merely admire him. He sat, looking down, with his head resting in his long, lean hand. That shock of dark hair, and beneath it, crystal blue eyes. Tall, lithe, and muscular. Will was at least ten years older and now a widower with two teenage girls to raise. Tierney reasoned she must be crazy, and what she was feeling was no more than repressed anger at the man who was holding her back from her rightful job. But every time she looked at Will Hutton, she saw only those eyes. She was so glad she kept these feelings to herself and denied them as often as possible.

Right now, Tierney had to convince Will Hutton that there

was a story that needed to be covered. Gathering her notebooks, along with her courage and resolve, Tierney marched into Will's office. He looked up and stared at her.

"Will, I've just interviewed Elizabeth Langford's daughter for my obit profile," Tierney said matter-of-factly.

"Doing what I hired you to do. Miracles never cease," Will mocked her. "I hate to ask, but why aren't you writing the story?"

"Uh, this is going to sound crazy. But stay with me here," Tierney said, launching into her idea.

Will turned and stood with his back to Tierney. "Jesus. Another of your conspiracies."

Unabated, Tierney pressed on. "Here's what I know. In the last six months, 29 otherwise healthy senior citizens have taken ill and have been admitted to the hospital. They get worse. Then, they all suddenly suffer from hallucinations, violent outbursts, then die. Why?" She tried to move in front of Will, who now faced the window, but he wouldn't budge.

Tierney pressed on. "Will, many of these people were healthy—a marathon runner, age 65. 72 - Senior Olympic Games. 63 taught gardening. They were all very active, then went downhill—hallucinations. Death. My gut says they are connected."

Will brushed past Tierney and slid into his chair. "Your gut? That's all you got. Not even enough. They're old. People do weird things before they die. And this began only after you started working here. Not before... hmmm. Yep, I'd say there's something going on all right." His voice had turned sarcastic. "Why did I ever let you come back here?"

Tierney ignored the question, which she interpreted as rhetorical. "These deaths are connected by one thing for sure. Doctor Nicholas "Briggs" Oxenbriggs. He's their doctor."

Will sighed and shook his head impatiently. "Tierney, you've been breathing in too much of the remaining coal dust. He is everybody's doctor in one way or another. Hell, Doc Briggs treated your grandmother. Was she one of his victims, too?"

Will slammed his fist down on his desk. "Tierney. You cannot use this paper or your position for some whacked-out revenge. Dr. Oxenbriggs did all he could—for your grandmother and even my—"

Tierney jumped but stood her ground. "Will. I am not on a vendetta. And I know Doc Briggs worked valiantly to save Mammaw and your wife. I know his whole history," Tierney began to recite in a lyrical fashion. "Briggs was an orphan kid in Massachusetts. Joined the military. Became a doctor, then started the rural health program in Dallas, Texas. Then came here by Lone Mountain Medical Center."

Will had tired of Tierney's constant drone of theories and wild ideas. He wanted her to know how ridiculous she sounded. "This is a remote mountain area. We are lucky to have him. What evil have you discovered about the good doctor? Medicare fraud? Prescription drug addiction? Mismatched ties and socks?"

"Be serious, Will," Tierney said. "Murder. This is about someone killing off patients, and the most likely suspect is either the great doctor or someone else at the hospital."

Will had lost all patience with Tierney. He abruptly stood, facing her, and Tierney's heart raced. He bellowed. "So, which is it? Dr. Briggs or the mysterious someone? Listen, I know you have a real flare for conspiracies, but this is crazy," Will stared down at Tierney. "If I catch you working on this at all, I will fire you—and no one will ever hire you in journalism again." "Will, please. I am not making this up. My Pappaw always says that numbers don't lie," Tierney hoped this would convince him to give credibility to her information. "And these numbers tell me that something is wrong."

Will dug in his heels. "But these numbers started only after you came here," Will said. "Can't you see what's going on? We are already on the edge with our few remaining advertisers, thanks to that Medicaid fraud story. The hospital buys a lot of ad space."

Tierney moved beside Will to face him, and then she placed a hesitant hand on his shoulder. He glared at her, and she withdrew her hand. Tierney wanted to tell him to trust her because she would never do anything to hurt him.

She wanted Will to know that she was glad to be working at the Daily Star, and because of him, she would never take any of the risks she had taken over in Knoxville. Instead, she tried to convince Will that she was just as dedicated to solid reporting as he was.

"Will, I know you are not afraid of doing hard-hitting, even controversial news stories," Tierney said. "That's how this paper has won so many awards and survived. So, what's this really about?"

Will nodded with a huff, and then he studied her face before he spoke in a deliberate, decisive tone.

"I believe in solid journalism—really well sourced stories—like the Medicaid story. That's why your 'theory' or 'hunch' is not worthy of our time. It's not news."

Tierney realized that she had to convince her no non-sense boss that she cared for the paper and its reputation. So, she told him that she loved the paper as much as he did and would not let anything happen to its well-earned cred-ibility. "Will, here's what I know. I've been tracking obits, you know. I've matched deaths to symptoms, and there's a pattern."

Will shook his head as he looked toward the ceiling. He now understood that he could not move Tierney from this crazy notion, but for the sake of the community, he had to try. He really wanted to help this waif of a girl who had some potential as a reporter, and for what he could pay, he needed her to rise to the challenge. Perhaps if he appealed to logic. What Will never realized was that if he had he asked Tierney Baynes, the woman almost 15 years his junior, to stop for him, she likely would have agreed. But Will had spent the last three years grieving the loss of his high school sweetheart. He looked down to his hand, the finger that still held his wedding ring. The man who prided himself on his keen powers of observation, was blind to Tierney's infatuation.

"Tierney, old people which we have many die," Will said. "Those numbers will be disproportionately higher than other areas. That's no story. Go find real news."

Tierney folded her arms and shook her head, not looking at Will. "But it could be more if you will authorize me to talk to some of the families. Do some research that goes back before I came. I won't tip anyone off. I promise. I also would like to see what kind of medicine was prescribed."

Tierney didn't move, didn't look at Will, didn't respond. Will spoke emphatically. "I will not, and you will leave this alone. This is not Knoxville. You say anything or start nosing around here and it's all over town. If I even suspect you are working on this, it will be your last day on the job."

Devastated, Tierney left the newsroom without a word. She didn't even acknowledge Emily, who had walked into the newsroom.

Down Wood Avenue at the police station, Eliot West

conducted a desperate search, one that would cost him this measly job if Sheriff Black caught him. Fortunately, the squad room was empty at lunch time. Eliot knew he had, at best, a couple of minutes. He was looking for any information on Doc Briggs, so he started with medical licenses. Briggs had one, but oddly, there were no deaths attributed to the great man's license. Eliot conducted the same search on chief resident, Ash McKay. To his shock, there were 21 deaths. Without more information, Eliot could not determine how the numbers were calculated, so even though 21 deaths in less than a year's work at Lone Mountain Medical Center sounded excessive, Eliot had no context. It could have been that Dr. McKay had signed 21 otherwise routine death certificates. Eliot needed more data. He had just uploaded another database when the bellowing voice of Sheriff Dove Black startled him.

Black would know Eliot was lying. The storied sheriff had a long history in Wise County and beyond. Certainly, there was crime in the mountains, domestic incidents, arguments that erupted in the bars around the edge of town, the occasional still that had to be demolished, illegal gambling, and a robbery here and there. However, in large part, the citizens lived in safety. That was even more so when the mines produced full-time, well-paying jobs. People slept with their doors unlocked. Neighbors supported one another.

In the public's eyes, Black was a warm, charming teddy

bear who remembered everyone's names, made sure shut-ins got hot meals and groceries, and had his staff do wellness checks without being asked. Black often said it's better to be friendly, to know what's going on, than it is to be called to the scene of a crime.

"I'm just a lazy, old coot," Black had been heard to say. "I'd much rather get to know everybody and their dogs before there's trouble. It's less work for me, and I get invited to a lot more Sunday dinners this way," Black chuckled.

What most people never knew, and those who did said nothing, was that Sheriff Black ran many of the illegal activities himself. He knew all the criminals, all the cons, and made quiet profits off all of them. This was an open secret among the officers on the force, and none of them ever crossed Sheriff Dove Black.

Eliot made it a point never to show how scared he was of Dove Black. That would have been a mistake. Black did not respect fear. He stomped into the squad room toward Eliot, who did not try to leave the computer. He knew Black would have it scanned to see the search history.

"West! Get the hell off that detective computer. What do you think you're doing? You are not a detective and cannot conduct investigations," Black ordered.

"Oh, Chief Black, I am not investigating just working a hunch about a doctor at the hospital. I think one of the residents or Doc Oxenbriggs—" Eliot tried to explain.

Black lumbered around behind the desk to loom over Eliot's shoulder. "You stop right there. That man is a saint. Saved my momma. Runs that free community clinic, trains every doctor coming and going. Gathers up all the family medical interns from the best schools to come to the RAM every year. Hell, he was a war hero. You have not been here long enough to accuse him of anything, and certainly not one of the residents he holds in regard."

Eliot knew it likely wouldn't work, but he tried to distract Sheriff Black. "RAM? Oh, yeah."

Black sounded even more irritated. "Don't act like you don't know what I mean. Remote Area Medical. With no union support or mining jobs, people can't afford good medical care. That guy from that TV show–er, Wild Kingdom–started it years ago, getting doctors, dentists, eye doctors–the works–to third world countries. But then he saw how great the need was in the United States."

Eliot was honestly perplexed. "What does that have to do with Briggs?"

With a single thumb, Sheriff Black pushed his hat further back on his head. "You are denser than mud. Briggs keeps that thing going here. Thousands of hurting people, waiting as much as three days in line for help they need but cannot afford."

Black recounted how Dr. Nicholas "Briggs" Oxenbriggs came to Wise County almost a decade earlier and saved it.

Sheriff Black said it was in the time when they couldn't get enough volunteer medical people to meet the demand for nearly 3,000 patients. Briggs had been in Wise County less than a year. "So, he just swung a wide net," Black recalled. "Here came all the residents, dental, and eye doctors from schools. All volunteers, and Briggs created a program that got them to stay." Sheriff Black had high praise for Oxenbriggs. "Even though Briggs has a full patient load at the hospital and runs the community clinics in Wise, Big Stone Gap, and Lee counties, he's the first doctor there and the last to leave."

Eliot realized he would have to have very hard evidence to get the Sheriff to change his mind, if he could do that at all. Eliot had hoped to do more investigating before he gave away all his information, but he needed the Sheriff to understand how serious this could be. He played his strongest hand.

"Sheriff Black, about Dr. Oxenbriggs... look what I found," Eliot pulled out his cell phone and flipped through the photos of his dad's medical chart. "He is prescribing a psychotic drug designed for people with schizophrenia to my dad. Given to a normal person, the drug will "

Black cut him off, and Eliot turned to face him. The sheriff's glare would have scared a lesser, unprepared person. But Eliot's dad was in danger, and notShing scared him more than that.

"If I catch or even think you are snooping around on Doctor "Briggs" Oxenbriggs or anybody he trusts, there won't be a municipality in the US of A that will hire you. Get out and go write parking tickets or help old ladies across the street." Black ordered Eliot, who still faced him.

The thick tension in the room was broken by the arrival of Barbara Patton, followed closely by several department employees returning from lunch. Spotting Sheriff Black, she approached him with a warm smile. Although he dreaded seeing the elegant woman, Black sported his warmest smile, walking back around the desk and toward Mrs. Patton with an outstretched hand, which she took graciously.

"Hello Sheriff Black. I am so glad to find you here. How are you?" Mrs. Patton asked.

"Mrs. Patton. I am quite well. And how are you holding up since your dear mother passed?" Sheriff Black paused just long enough to give Mrs. Patton time to take a deep breath. "I hated to hear we lost such a wonderful lady and that she was working on a new trail just before she took ill."

Barbara nodded, displaying a warm smile. "Oh, thank you, Sheriff. That's so kind of you to say. I know your wife helped her with the senior classes so many times."

That told Sheriff Black that Mrs. Patton was on her game. She could recall specific personal details about his family. "Nice of you to remember," he said warmly. "I'm sure you came to check on the investigation into your mother's ruby broach, and I am sad to report that we have not found anyone who even saw it after she was admitted. Are you sure she wore it on her trail walk that day? Have you searched her apartment?"

Mrs. Patton nodded in response to each of his questions, finally adding that her mother always wore the broach, despite her warnings, and her children and husband had gone through her mother's house, belongings, and car several times. She said they had also posted lost and found notices on several websites to no avail. "That morning, when Mother met me for breakfast, she was wearing the broach on her sweater. I had a safety pin, and so I pinned it an extra time to be sure. Can you check with the hospital again, please? They are not returning my calls. I've become a thorn in their side, I fear," Mrs. Patton said in her most charming voice.

Barbara Patton had learned many years ago that to get men in this part of the Commonwealth to help you, you had to appear to need their help, disarm them, and then cut to the jugular. She had walked into that station with a singular agenda—to get someone to take responsibility and action in the search for her mother's broach. But Mrs. Patton realized, of course, that she could not simply ask for that. She would have to find a way to put the great Sheriff Dove Black in a position where yes was the only answer. As she walked toward the sheriff's office just a few minutes ago, she had seen Sheriff Black in some sort of confrontation with Eliot West. That gave her the answer she needed. Barbara knew all the rumors about Sheriff Dove Black's criminal sideline enterprises. She also knew that Etta West's son had been a decent detective in Knoxville.

Now, she set her trap. Sheriff Black looked at her with soft eyes. "Mrs. Patton, of course we won't stop looking. You can count on that. We have only one detective. Bear with us." Sheriff Black said in his most charming, reassuring tone.

Barbara Patton sighed. "Well, Sheriff, I don't mean to get into your operation, but what about this young man?" She turned to Eliot West, who gave her a quizzical look.

"You're Etta West's son, right? We're in the garden club together. Eliot is it?"

"Yes, ma'am. I could—" Eliot started to speak, but the sheriff cut him off.

"Uh, Mrs. Patton, he's just joined the force and not a detective yet."

"Sheriff, you would not hire an unqualified officer, I'm sure," Barbara said confidently. "And if you need extra hands, I'm sure Etta's boy would be more than happy to help you in this situation."

"Of course, I would," Eliot saw his opportunity and was not going to let go.

"Uh, Mrs. Patton, I'll give your wonderful idea due

consideration," Sheriff Black tried to close the idea as softly as he knew how.

Barbara Patton was just getting started. "Sheriff, I understand, and I expect to see this young man working on the case," she said with a warm, confident smile. "I will call in a few days. Meanwhile, Eliot, please come by the house, and I will fill you in on what we've done so far. I also have some apple butter for your mother. My husband and I will be ready to help any way we can," Barbara offered genuinely. She gave the sheriff a look that he took to mean he had no option. With a wave, she turned and left the office. Once outside and making certain that the sheriff could not see her face, Barbara Patton said to herself, "Game. Set. Match."

Meanwhile, Eliot watched the sheriff's face. He was calculating his next step carefully. Eliot realized that the Sheriff was really in a bind. He realized that through her husband, Mrs. Patton held an independent power that even the high sheriff could not surpass. Her husband was publisher of the mighty Kingsport newspaper. The sheriff knew he had to keep on Mrs. Patton's good side. He quickly calculated his options. If he did as Mrs. Patton requested, then the great man would not be completely in control. If he did not follow her request, then the consequences could mean Sheriff Dove Black might no longer be able to keep his criminal activities in the dark. If Eliot thought the sheriff would honor Mrs. Patton's request, he was about to be disappointed. Black turned to him and growled his decision.

"I don't care if her husband is the Pope. You're not getting involved. You hear me?"

Eliot stood silent for a moment, then said, "She will be expecting me—and so will he."

That must have caught Black off-guard because he said nothing. Eliot took the silence to continue. "Her husband is the editor of the Kingsport Times Courier, and he could investigate this himself or send reporters if he thought there was anything to it."

Watching the sheriff's red face, Eliot thought he was on a winning streak, so he proceeded. "And if I don't show up—no telling what he might think is worth investigating."

The sheriff stared hard at Eliot, perhaps trying to intimidate him, perhaps hoping the younger man would back down.

"There ain't nothing for him to find," Sheriff Black declared. He paused for another second, and then to Eliot's surprise, he relented. "But all right—go over there, but stick to a missing ruby broach—nothing else, and bring me a jar of that apple butter."

CHAPTER 9
Secret Questions

Dr. Ash McKay secreted a stack of patient charts from their holders behind the nurses' station. Fortunately, he had picked the very moment when the four nurses on duty had either gone on break or were with patients. He hurriedly headed toward the old, empty wing and a vacant patient room. Piling the charts onto an old, dusty desk and grabbing his pen, McKay quickly scanned the files, looking for a singular entry—the Haldol prescription. He pulled out his cell phone and snapped photos. Then, he pulled a legal pad from the bottom of the stack, and he began to write instructions for the nurses to stop the prescriptions. He then snapped photos of the instructions.

McKay had learned from one of the nurses that Dr. Oxenbriggs never wrote his own orders. Instead, he would write them on legal pads, have a nurse type them, and then destroy the legal pad notes.

"It's fool proof," McKay said. "Since Briggs has the nurses type in his orders, they will just think this is more of his notes for them to do. There's no way for him, or them, to know I did this," McKay hoped he would be correct.

As he was gathering the charts and notes, McKay realized exactly where he was. This was the room to which he had seen Briggs retreat recently. He wondered why this room and what could be here that lured the great man to this space. McKay began to look around. He pulled open drawers to find nothing at all. He looked around, spotting an old night stand with a drawer. He tried that one to find it empty as well. McKay was frustrated, upset with himself for even thinking Dr. Oxenbriggs was doing something evil. The only proof he had were those prescriptions, and those were not definitive. After all, McKay didn't know the patients; perhaps there was a reason for the Haldol.

He had almost convinced himself that he was wrong when he noticed that the night stand drawer stood slightly ajar. He tried to push it closed, but it wouldn't budge. After several attempts, McKay shoved the drawer with all his strength, but it refused to close. He realized there must be something blocking the drawer, so McKay shined the flashlight on his phone into the dark crevice.

At first, he saw nothing, but as he maneuvered the light a bit deeper, something reflected. Crouching lower, McKay tried to open the drawer and close it again. This time, he heard the sound as the back of the drawer smacked something hard and probably metal. McKay pulled out the night stand and examined it from the back. It appeared to be solid wood. He couldn't break it without someone noticing that. McKay lifted the night stand and shook it. To his amazement, a metal box fell to the floor, spilling its contents on the floor. He frantically tried to catch them, stop them from rolling, and then gathered them up and carefully set the ancient box on top of the desk, alongside the charts.

Lockets, bracelets, insignia rings, rings with initials inside, lapel pins, lockets, and chains. Each item was tagged and numbered, all in the same deep, indigo ink and carefully crafted, block letters. McKay snapped photos of the box, the night stand, and as many of the items as he could frantically collect and position in a few minutes. McKay knew his time was running out, and he would have to leave. They would be missing him on the floor.

He struggled with the night stand from the front, but eventually found the small cavity that served as a hiding place and slid the box back into it. He closed the drawer, moved back to the desk, gathered up his notes and the charts, and started to exit the room. That's when he heard the footsteps echoing on the tiles outside the room. Someone was coming this way. Dr. McKay had to find a place to hide. He found a tiny crevice behind the dusty, no-longer-white curtain that divided the room from ceiling to floor. Quickly, McKay stood motionless behind the curtain. He tried not to breathe.

Suddenly, with a heavy groan, Dr. Oxenbriggs flopped

into the chair where McKay had just been. McKay squirmed in the tight space to turn off his phone so that he could see what Briggs was doing. Then, he noticed the stack of charts on the floor behind Oxenbriggs. He tried to figure out a way to get them, but each time he moved, Oxenbriggs seemed to hear the sound.

Finally, McKay resigned himself to the crevice and watched as Oxenbriggs stood, walked ever too close to him, and retrieved the metal box from the night stand. He opened it and lovingly picked out pieces of jewelry. Oxenbriggs took a blank label from his pocket. Then, he drew a ruby broach from his jacket pocket, tied a label to it, and placed the broach into the box. He stared at it for a moment, then removed the broach and pulled off the tag. He dropped both into his breast pocket. He closed the box but thought something about it felt odd. So, Briggs held the box up to the light and examined it. Finding nothing obvious, he shook his head, then rubbed a hand lovingly over the box. Then, he stood and walked back toward the night stand, where he appeared to be staring straight at Ash McKay, who held his breath so as not to move the curtain. Briggs shrugged and then deftly replaced the box back into its hiding place and closed the drawer.

Briggs turned and plodded to the desk, where he flopped into the chair. Then, he pulled open what appeared to be an ordinary, empty drawer. However, he lifted a false bottom and retrieved a scrapbook. Opening it, he ran his hands along the thickness of the pages, then flipped through them. Near the front of the book, Briggs stopped on an empty, black page. Then, he carefully pulled what appeared to be a newspaper clipping from the inside pocket of his lab coat and unfolded it.

When Briggs paused to read the article, Ash McKay breathed softly, still fearing he would be caught. He had stood stiffly so long that he could no longer feel his feet, and his calves throbbed. Sharp pains cut his head in half, and his arms felt as if each one weighed tons. Yet, he forced himself to remain motionless. Unwillingly, Ash's eyes closed for the briefest of moments. It must have been then that Briggs did something with the clipping. For when Ash focused again, Briggs no longer held the paper, and the scrapbook was closed. As Ash watched, Briggs closed the drawer and stood. He spoke in a loving, yet odd-sounding tone, as if he were speaking to a memory.

"My dear Mrs. Langford," Briggs began, "I will carry you with me forever. I know you are at peace now. I would have taken great pleasure in spending more time with you - watching the peace of death come over your face." Then, his voice changed back to the officious Briggs that Ash had come to know. "Well, more work to do."

Ash realized that the usually observant Oxenbriggs had not seen the stack of medical charts that were stacked so close to the desk. Ash considered that for a while, then concluded that Oxenbriggs must be so intent on whatever it was that he had hidden in this room, that nothing else mattered. "This is not like him," Ash thought. "Something is definitely wrong, but what?"

Ash was so engrossed with analyzing the options for answering that question that he did not hear Briggs push back the chair, rise, walk to the door, open it, and walk out. It was only when Briggs reached back inside the room, near the door, and clicked off the light that Ash realized he was alone with the shadows in the room. Not trusting the silence, Ash stood still for what seemed like an eternity. When he was certain that Briggs had really gone, Ash let out a heavy sigh, stretched out fully, shook the pain from his arms and legs, and moved his neck from side to side. Then, he quickly tip-toed to the desk. Using his phone's soft light, Ash fiddled with the drawer until it opened. To his shock, the scrapbook was deceptively thin.

Obituaries of local residents filled page after page. Organized like a medical chart, the oldest were at the back and the most recent on the front pages. The one on top was none other than Mrs. Elizabeth Langford, the prominent leader of so many civic initiatives in Wise and Lee counties, who had passed away recently. Ash recalled her because he was on call the day she died, and he signed her death certificate. The nurses had found Mrs. Langford on their rounds.

Ash rushed in with the team and tried to resuscitate her, which was the protocol. She was already dead.

As Ash closed the book, he thought he heard a noise in the hallway, so he frantically slid the book into the hidden compartment and closed the drawer. He listened to the silence for a moment, then hurriedly gathered up the charts and headed out of the dark room.

Quickening his pace as he entered the bustling, brightly lit main hallway, Ash tried to shake off his jitters, hoping no one would notice how rattled he was. He tried to breathe, to walk normally, but he could feel his heart pounding. As he turned toward the nurses' station, Ash felt his body relax and thought he was safe. But the buzz of his cell phone in his jacket pocket startled him.

Ash glanced around, looking for a place to unload the charts to grab the phone. He found a computer stand, where he slid the charts, and one clattered to the floor. Ash made the quick choice to grab his phone and answer breathlessly. He did not recognize the voice but immediately wished he had just kept walking. He tried to crouch into a corner to listen.

"Hello," a perky, if somewhat rushed voice spilled out words one on top of another. "My name is Tierney Baynes, and I am a reporter with the Big Stone Gap Daily Star."

"How did you get this number?" an irritated Ash McKay demanded.

"The switchboard patched me through to you," Tierney explained.

"I'll have to remember to thank them," McKay could not hide his sarcasm.

Tierney didn't seem to notice Ash's anger or the sarcasm. She blubbered on. "I am working on a profile of Elizabeth Langford, who died last week. I understand you were treating her."

Ash was listening carefully and didn't like what he was hearing. "You're writing a story–about a dead person? I'd say that's really digging for news. Anyway, I cannot help you at all," he tried to brush her off.

Undeterred, Tierney pushed on without invitation. "How about I buy you a cup of coffee?" She waited for a moment in silence. She knew that always made people uncomfortable because they felt the need to fill the silence.

Ash tried for a lighter tone. "Residents drink too much coffee, and we never have time to sit down. Why don't you talk to her family?" He realized this bulldog of a reporter was not going away.

"I have already, and they asked me to talk to you as well," Tierney said flatly. "Said you were very touched by her death."

Ash shook his head and sighed. "Death is always hard, and I feel for the families who lose loved ones," he said in all sincerity.

"So, how about her death in particular?" Tierney asked. "Was it harder than others you've experienced?"

It suddenly occurred to Ash that this reporter might be recording their conversation, and he never wanted anything to do with any news story. "You are not recording me or writing this down, are you? I am not speaking to you for the record."

Tierney was accustomed to that question, and she had grown accustomed to her canned response. "No, Dr. McKay. I would not be underhanded like that," she responded. She tried another tactic that usually worked. "I just have a positive story to write about a remarkable woman. You were with her in her last day, that's all."

Tierney waited again to see whether the doctor would take her bait. Ash glanced nervously, looking down the hallway that had filled with patients, staff, and visitors. He would have to conclude this conversation. He just wanted this conversation to end.

"Is that all?" Ash huffed. "I have nothing to tell you about Mrs. Langford—or any other patients who have died. So, I need to conclude this conversation, Ms. Baynes."

Tierney could not believe what he had said. "Other patients who died!" Tierney tried to hold her excitement. Finally, someone in authority who could corroborate her suspicions. She needed to keep this conversation going.

Ash realized he had said too much. "Ms. Baynes. I need

to go. Unfortunately, death is a part of what we face here," he didn't think for a second that his attempt at backtracking worked.

Tierney pressed on. "Dr. McKay, just one question," Tierney could not hide her excitement. "How many of the others seemed to die too young, too quickly and were experiencing some sort of hallucinations—seeing things that weren't there?"

An astonished Ash McKay nearly dropped the phone, and he was sure she heard him gasp. Someone outside the hospital—a reporter of all people—knew something was wrong. He wondered what exactly she knew. For a split second, Ash thought about asking that very question, but he had heard the stories about this reporter. He tried to control his curiosity and end the conversation.

"Where did you hear that?" Ash exclaimed, then paused. "I have to go now. Don't call me again."

Tierney tried one more tactic—the standard face-to-face meeting. "Dr. McKay, if you will trust me. Just agree to meet me—off-site—away from town," she listened, hoping the silence meant Ash McKay would agree. She was wrong.

"Trust you!" Ash exclaimed in a fervent whisper. "Ha! I know what happens when a person trusts you. They find themselves facing jail time because you've inflated the amount of illegal booze and marijuana they sold. A misdemeanor becomes a felony. Yeah, I'm sure I can trust you," he could not hide his anger.

"Dr. McKay, you've been talking to Eliot West," Tierney said. "You've put your money on the wrong horse for sure."

Dr. McKay angrily pushed the end button on the call, shoved the phone back into his pocket, and started to stomp off. Then, he remembered the charts and rushed back to get them. Stopping to take a deep breath and arrange the charts so he could carry them calmly, Ash told himself that he had not said too much and that the awful reporter would go after someone else. Feeling once again in control, Ash took two steps down the hallway and slammed directly into Dr. Oxenbriggs, who was turning the corner and reading something on his cell phone. Surprised, but cheerful, Briggs pushed Ash back with one hand on his shoulder and a charming smile.

"Slow down." Briggs said in a lyrical, calm voice, "And what were you doing coming from that direction? And what about all these charts, and where were you coming from?"

Caught off-guard, Ash stumbled for a moment, "Uh, oh, needed a quiet place to think, and that wing is not used. So, it's my respite."

He waited while Oxenbriggs considered the explanation, staring at Ash as if he were analyzing a patient. This made Ash squirm. Finally, Oxenbriggs spoke in his calm, controlled voice.

"Are you okay, Ash? Some young doctors think that

community medicine will be less pressure than a specialty. I know in your case, you were headed toward cardiology before you responded to my call and came to the RAM for three years," Oxenbriggs was conciliatory, almost loving.

This made Ash want to confess, to explain how worried he had become over the patient treatment plans, how scared he was that his own career was in jeopardy, how he feared he had said too much to the reporter. But the scientist in Ash held him back, saved him from himself. Later, he would be thankful. All he could muster was a weak agreement with Dr. Briggs.

"Uh, you're right about that, Doc Briggs," Ash said with a deep breath. "Community medicine is demanding. Especially when you lose patients," Ash said.

"Mrs. Langford? You cannot blame yourself," Dr. Briggs offered.

"I, uh, don't. She was already gone when I got to the room," Ash relaxed a little.

"Oh, that is good." Dr. Briggs retained his calm, caring composure. "I mean, many's a young doctor who never recovers from a loss," Briggs said. He patted Ash's shoulder, then dropped his hand.

"What? Are you saying that I was responsible for her death?" Any calm that Ash had regained drained out of him.

"Your name is on the death certificate," Briggs was accusing Ash, still in that loving, calm voice that Ash was beginning to hate.

"That's just a formality," Ash was shocked.

"Not to her family," Briggs said.

Ash felt like a fly in a spider's web. "Dr. Oxenbriggs. Mrs. Langford was dead when I entered her room. There was nothing I could do for her at that point. She had a 'Do Not Resuscitate,' as well. Do YOU think I could have done something more," Ash scrambled to defend himself.

Dr. Oxenbriggs maintained that sickeningly cool demeanor and calming voice. Only his eyes gave away his cold, emotionless interior.

"Mrs. Langford's family is grieving," Dr. Oxenbriggs said. "They want to blame someone. It's not unusual, and your name is on the death certificate."

Ash felt compelled to defend himself. "I did my best and signed a death certificate," Ash was astonished. "There is no liability, Dr. Briggs." Then, he thought of something he could do. It was a risk for sure, but Ash had to make the good doctor aware that he was not going to be the only one blamed.

"One thing I know for sure," Ash said. "Her entire treatment plan and our credentials will be laid out for all the public to see. It will not be just what happened on the day Mrs. Langford died."

Ash watched Briggs carefully for any sign that the remark had an impact. Boy, Briggs was practiced and smooth. But

Ash saw one tiny twitch in Briggs' eyes.

"How do you figure that?" Briggs asked.

Ash gained a little more confidence and pressed ahead. "In court, it's all public, and they will go over her treatment, her medications, her history, and our qualifications in great detail."

Ash stood facing Oxenbriggs, who gave away little. After a moment, Briggs spoke. "I will talk to the family and let them know you did all you could. Meanwhile, I can put those charts where they go."

Briggs smiled and started to walk past Ash, but stopped, turned, and looked at Ash with a comforting smile. He pointed to the charts in Ash's arm.

"You really shouldn't be taking those away from the desk or the patients' room, Dr. McKay. I'd be happy to put them back for you."

"Oh, sir. I am sorry," Ash said. "I was reviewing your treatment plans, trying to learn how you think. I needed a quiet place."

Dr. Briggs' look turned to ice. "Well, next time, just ask me."

Ash hurried to the nurses' station and quickly slid each chart into its slot on the wall. He raced off toward the stairwell, where he knew he could make a phone call.

"We have to talk," he whispered into his cell phone. "Yeah, tonight at the Mutual."

CHAPTER 10
Pieces of the Puzzle

After dark, there wasn't much traffic on Wood Avenue, especially on a weeknight. Eliot was always concerned that Sheriff Dove Black would somehow know he had come there to meet Dr. Ash McKay. That would cost Eliot his meager job and end any hope he had of finding out what was happening to his dad. Ash McKay stepped cautiously, making sure he remained in the shadow of the single-story buildings that lined the street. Eliot felt McKay moving slowly, but stood motionless until McKay faced him.

"West, have you been talking to that reporter, Tierney Baynes?" Ash practically accused the police officer. "She called me today, out of the blue, asking about patients with hallucinations, memory loss, and unusual problems."

Eliot shook his head. "I don't talk to that bitch!"

"Well, she got her information from somewhere!" Ash said angrily.

"Not me," West said flatly. "Is that what you called me for—to accuse me of talking to a reporter? If so, then we have nothing to say. I want to help my dad, that's all."

Ash shook his head. "No, no. I found something, and I think it's evidence you can investigate."

Eliot had a slightly quizzical look, but he still intimidated McKay. "Look, doc. I've told you I cannot investigate anything."

"But it's a room in the old wing of the hospital," Ash could not stop. "Briggs goes there to decompress, I suppose. But I found his stash of jewelry from patients and a scrapbook of news clippings about patients who have died."

Eliot was angry. "You expect me to believe this? Doc Briggs has some sort of mementos from patients stashed in an empty room in the hospital. Maybe the patients gave them to him as gifts and he doesn't want them in his house."

"I tell you, there is a box and clippings and a note that says, "Death is my gift to you."

Eliot had to have proof. "Look, it may seem strange to you, but it's not a crime as far as I can see. You have to give me more," Eliot said flatly.

Ash struggled to think of a way to get Eliot to understand what he found and what it could mean. "He was talking to himself—saying how he was sorry he missed seeing a patient die."

Eliot paused for a moment. "That may be weird, for sure. But—"

"Mrs. Langford—that's who he said. Mrs. Langford," Ash said almost triumphantly.

"Tell me what he said, exactly," Eliot said.

"Uh, let's see. He said something about how he missed her passing but that he knows she is now peaceful," Ash rushed through the words, "and uh, then he said he would have her with him forever."

"How did you come by this information?" Eliot asked suspiciously.

"I am a researcher at heart, Eliot," Ash explained. "So, I went to investigate the room on the unused hall where Dr. Oxenbriggs goes off to sometimes. He came in, and I hid. I couldn't see him well, but I could hear him clearly. Now, you can go get a search warrant or something, right?"

"No. I cannot. There's nothing that even suggests a crime," Eliot thought he had said this before. "And if there were, you just put yourself right in the middle. You left behind prints, DNA. For a guy who calls himself a researcher, you didn't handle this like a science investigation."

Ash McKay was frustrated, but not defeated. He pulled out his iPhone and slid his index finger through a series of photos. "Here, look. I took photos."

Eliot took the phone and studied each photo. He flicked a few buttons to send the images to himself, then handed the phone back to McKay.

"Well?" Ash asked with a great sense of anticipation. "You have the evidence."

Eliot shook his head. "I cannot use this or even mention

it. And now that your fingerprints are all over everything, a good criminal defense lawyer—and I'm sure the hospital can get one—would not let this get to court. There is one thing. Did you happen to notice if there was a piece of jewelry with Mrs. Langford when she died, or did you see that with his collection?"

The question took Ash by surprise. "What? No. There wasn't." He explained that the family and hospital security already asked about the broach. "I couldn't see what he placed into the box and didn't get a chance to look after he left. You can go look—investigate."

Eliot was getting tired of McKay's insistence that the officer investigate. "Back to that again. If it's there, who's to say you didn't drop it there to incriminate an innocent man?"

Ash paced in the dark shadows. A car drove by slowly. Eliot watched it go and then turn right on First Street by the Southwest Virginia Museum. There were lots of homes in that direction, so he figured it was somebody heading home. Then, Ash spoke in a voice that was filled with desperation and frustration.

"Damn!" Ash demanded "Try to do the right thing. You know I was going into cardiology—then, at Coastal Virginia Medical University, I saw this opportunity to spend a semester—tuition free—in community medicine. So, I took it. I came here for three years—working at the RAM. I had never seen such need or met such incredible people. They withstood every hardship with resilience and strength. I wanted to help them, to learn from them.

Finally met Doc Briggs, and it changed my whole direction. The people in need—the wonderful people who were stronger and braver than anyone I had ever met. Doc Briggs—a hero to everyone here. I cannot believe I'm even thinking about him in a sinister way.'"

Eliot had listened to Ash's long treatise about his motivation for being in Southwest Virginia. He hoped he could now get Ash to talk about Ira West and help him.

"Look, you're right about one thing. Our people are the best in the world, and they deserve the best," Eliot said. "Listen, do you have any news on my dad?"

Ash had found the way to get Eliot to act. "Think about your dad. He has so much life to live."

"Why don't you just get word to the medical authorities?" Eliot asked. "If Oxenbriggs is doing something medially wrong? Is he hurting my father?"

"Tall order, Eliot," Ash said. "I cannot go to the medical authorities on the information I have."

"Listen, why don't you anonymously mail his orders to the medical authorities. Does he sign them?" Eliot asked.

Ash nodded. "Sometimes. Sometimes, he has the nurses stamp his signature on the pages they type up for him. He doesn't hand write his own orders," Ash explained.

"That makes it tougher. Mail them, and if knowledgeable

medical authorities review them, they can do something. This is not a police matter. The only thing I'm interested in is that ruby broach," Eliot said. "And my dad? How is he?"

"What about your dad?" Ash asked. "This medication will take its toll, and the more he takes, the less time he has. He won't be able to survive it. Each time, he will get weaker and less in control. He will not be able to eat. What began as a very mild and easily survivable stroke will end with–"

Eliot interrupted the doctor. "Stop! I will do all I can to help my dad, but you've spoiled any potential police investigation with your snooping." Eliot said. Then, he looked up and down the empty street, glanced at his watch, and put his hat on his head. "I have to get back on patrol."

A few hours later, Emily Scott and Tierney Baynes walked along a stretch of Wood Avenue toward the library on the upper end of town. They had come from the new, trendy coffee shop that filled an old storefront on the far end of Wood Avenue. Most of the public never knew that reporters who worked at morning daily papers rarely came into the office before 11 a.m. or left before Midnight. That's why seeing this pair on the street early should have set off alarms that they were working on a big story.

For most morning daily newspapers, the staff worked shifts that began in the late morning and ended in the late evening hours. That's why it was unusual for the two

Daily Star reporters to be on the job before 10 a.m. But no one they passed along the street knew the hours journalists kept.

Working most nights until nearly midnight when the last story was "put to bed," no self-respecting journalist ever came to work before 11 the next morning. However, Emily and Tierney were on an important mission—to spend as much time as possible mining the databases at the public library.

"I just cannot believe more people—ordinary citizens—aren't lined up to research these gold mines of information," Tierney exclaimed.

"I don't know if all this information should be publicly available," Emily mused. "But when I need it, I'm sure glad it is! Now let's get there quickly, T."

This morning, Tierney and Emily were hoping to find some information on the history of the ruby broach that was missing from the effects of Elizabeth Langford. They knew that the one and only Gilley's Jewelry Store, still in business today, made Mrs. Langford's broach in 1960 for her birthday. Her husband surprised her with the piece at a time when they had no extra money. He had saved and saved. Both Tierney and Emily agreed that was interesting, but they needed more to come up with a front page story. Short of someone confessing to a theft, they agreed they had no real hook.

Emily stopped and faced Tierney. "Here's an angle. The broach was a one-of-a-kind piece. It's what—60 years old or so, making it even more valuable, and I don't think it's missing. I think whoever took it is keeping it for themselves."

"So, why haven't we seen it at any of the pawn shops, or even on the online classifieds?" Tierney exclaimed.

"I wonder if the police are thinking along those lines." Emily said and almost immediately wished she could retract her words.

Tierney was off on a new, unrealistic direction. "Now, we're thinking. So, let's go to the sheriff's office and see if we can charm anything out of the detective."

Emily knew they had little time to get to the library, conduct the research, and still do their other four stories that were due that evening. Will would be unforgiving. "Tierney, wait a minute. We need to get to the library right now," Emily hoped her appeal worked. "And what happens if the detective is not there or we ask and get nothing? Then, we've played our hand to no avail."

"Okay, I see your point," Tierney said.

Emily thought Tierney gave in way too easily, and that made Emily suspicious. "So, what have you been checking on our databases about Dr. Briggs already? What did you find out about our beloved doctors? Spill now while we are out of the newsroom."

Tierney blurted out an answer before she thought.

"Geeze! You never let up. Okay. Ash McKay is straight-forward. Hails from New York state. No record. Excelled in medical school in Coastal Virginia. Worked RAM a few semesters and was among the six senior residents hand-picked by Briggs to participate in the community medicine program. If he passes, he will work in a rural setting for four years and have most of his student loans paid off by the community."

Emily pressed on. "And the great man himself? I suppose he has impeccable credentials."

Tierney was so eager to tell what she knew. "That's the thing. I had trouble finding him. Seems there are two Nicholas Oxenbriggs. One died the year ours was born. Sounds like identity theft to me."

Emily thought it was time to rein her fellow reporter in a bit. "Tierney. That's ridiculous. Even if Briggs could steal an identity, he couldn't steal all the medical credentials and training. AGH!"

The two were so engrossed in their conversation, they failed to see Sheriff Dove Black lumbering quietly toward them. To no one's surprise, he had heard most of their conversation, but in typical fashion for the infamous sheriff, he pretended he had not heard a word. He tipped his hat to Tierney and Emily, who smiled. Emily put on her best little girl face, which she used to disarm officials.

"Well, good day, members of the press," Sheriff Black

said sweetly. "What salacious story are you two working on today?" He made it sound like he had offered them lemonade on a hot day.

Emily spoke first, matching the sheriff's tone. "Hello, Sheriff. We're just about to head to the library to work on boring research. Nothing exciting at all."

To Emily's chagrin, Tierney blurted out, "Yes, but we were going to stop by your office first."

"Oh, and why would that be?" the sheriff crooned.

Tierney blurted on, her words tumbling clumsily out. "You know that ruby broach that went missing after the death of Elizabeth Langford? We just wanted a status on the investigation." She smiled.

The sheriff would give away nothing. "We have that well in hand, well in hand."

Tierney took that to mean the investigation had been concluded. "So then, you have found the broach?"

Sheriff Black cut her off softly. "We are working the case, and Ms. Baynes, you would do well not to let your imagination get the best of you and say too much that you cannot prove—especially when it involves prominent citizens."

At this moment, Emily realized that the sheriff had heard their conversation. She wondered what he really thought and what would be the consequences for the newspaper. She discreetly tugged at Tierney's shirt sleeve, but Tierney kept blundering on with a sideways warning. Emily wanted to disappear and feared they might if her fellow reporter kept on. Tierney chattered on, unfazed.

"That is good advice, Sheriff. Thank you." Tierney said. "Some prominent citizens think they are above the law, too."

Here came the warning, and Emily knew it.

"You'd do well to keep to the facts missy. There ain't criminals behind every tree around here. This is a safe community because we keep it that way. So, don't go borrowing trouble." With a long, hard stare behind his charming smile, Sheriff Dove Black lumbered off toward the police department.

Emily had long known that Sheriff Dove Black ruled by intimidation and kept the peace in the remote mountains through a variety of protection schemes for businesses. His take of the local illegal gambling came right off the top.

"Tierney, he must have heard us. Geez!" Emily said in a loud whisper.

Tierney was undeterred. "He doesn't scare me. My Pappaw said Sheriff Black has his hands in everything crooked in this whole area. We can hold that over his head if he gets out of line." With that, Tierney marched forward toward the upper end of town and the library.

Emily shook her head in exasperation. She realized her childhood friend would always possess both the naivety and magical thinking of a child. She had to try and get a warning into that thick head. "And people who cross him tend to leave town, never to return, if you know what I mean.

But, there's never any proof. T—you must not go after him," Emily warned.

Tierney ignored her. "Oh, be serious, will you! I don't go after people. I pursue story ideas," Tierney proclaimed.

"In your case, those are one in the same," Emily growled.

The pair walked in silence for a moment, enjoying the crisp air. Then, Tierney blurted out. "Hey, you still sort of like Eliot West, don't you? Why don't you invite him for coffee?"

Emily's face knotted into a combination of annoyed and exasperated. Tierney took their friendship for granted, and Emily knew exactly what Tierney wanted her to do. "You are lower than low. He will not rat on the sheriff. He knows the stakes."

Tierney shook her head and waved a defiant hand in the air. "Don't be silly. Ask him about the broach investigation. Tell him how much I annoy you. He hates me."

Emily jumped right back. "And not without reason after what you did to him in Knoxville."

"Oh, not that again! So, I messed up a few numbers and dollar signs," Tierney brushed off the incident. "He was the one selling evidence. But if you can talk to him now, we may get more on this story."

Tierney had tried, unsuccessfully, to persuade Emily. "You cost him his job—and only afterward did the police internal affairs investigation show the numbers were way below what you reported," Emily stated. "Doesn't that bother you?"

The pair had stopped walking, and Tierney began to pace. "Now you're defending him! Will you talk to him—soon, please?"

Emily wanted Tierney to focus on the task they had before them. She wanted Tierney to essentially grow up, but after all these years as friends, Emily thought that was a lost cause. So, for the moment, she wanted Tierney to let her be. "I'll try. If you will promise me you won't try to investigate the sheriff. I'd like to live—here."

They made their way to the library and came away with less than they had anticipated but more than they realized. At least they had enough to finish the last installment of the Medicaid story. It seemed the doctor had spent the money he pocketed on a resort home in Lake Tahoe, a nice boat, and a tiny beach condo at Myrtle Beach.

A few days later, the entire street was abuzz with conversations about the final installment of the Medicaid fraud story that appeared on the front page of the Big Stone Gap Daily Star. Leaving the Mutual with his coffee, Dr. Oxenbriggs had hoped to get to the hospital without too many interruptions from townspeople. But that was not to be. As he slid out the door, Briggs was stopped by Jesse and his friend, Web. These two were closer than brothers, having worked for years together in the mines. There, they learned to depend upon their coworkers for safety, for support in the darkness underground, and often for survival.

Jesse's wife left him several years back for what she thought would be a better future in Chicago. She had taken their two children, and Jesse had not seen them since. Web, on the other hand, had a wife and two grown children. After the mines closed, he found work doing odd jobs and working in a building supply store. His children were in college, and his wife was not accustomed to having her husband underfoot during the day. So, when he wasn't working, Web found Jesse, and they caught up just like the old days.

That morning, when he saw Doc Briggs coming out of the Mutual, Jesse shoved the paper at him.

"Hey, Doc Briggs. Look at this," he said. "You'll want to be here for this one."

The title read: TV Network to do Story on Remote Area Medical Clinic

Before Doc Briggs could read farther, Web interrupted. "Will you be interviewed? You're going to be a star, and it will be on WCYB-TV. Next thing, CNN will be in town. This will put us on the map."

Briggs was taken aback by the thoughts of television, something he did not want at all. He tried to retain his cool composure. "You really think national news would be interested in this story?"

"I do believe they will be," Web proudly announced. "No

other place in the country has anything like RAM. That's what the paper says."

Doc Briggs shook his head and pressed the paper back toward Jesse, who gestured no with both palms. "No, Doc, you keep it. And I am sure you will be on TV after all you've done for this community."

Oxenbriggs handed the paper to Web and tried to find an appropriately demure response. "I've done nothing, guys." He hoped his hands did not shake and reveal how nervous he really was. The last thing Nicholas Oxenbriggs wanted was the limelight shined upon him.

Web spoke first, trying to cajole the great man into accepting the idea of speaking for the community and getting some well-earned attention. "C'mon, Doc. Don't tell me you're camera shy. When they get here, I'm going to find them reporters and give 'em good news about our great doctor who brought good health and medical training to these mountains."

Doc Briggs stepped off the curb, hoping to make a clean get away to the safety of his truck. "Ah, no. Don't go bringing my name into this. Anyway, I have a medical conference coming up. Likely somewhere else when they get here." Although he didn't have a conference scheduled, there were always half a dozen each month, and Briggs was certain he could find one that would keep him out of town for a week. Since television people tended to swoop in and out like vultures, that would be more than enough time.

Jesse tried once more to convince Briggs. "Well, all the good you do here would make a great story, Doc. You deserve it."

"I have no story to tell. Now, I must get to the hospital," Briggs scurried across Wood Avenue to his truck and drove away toward the hospital.

Jesse and Web watched him go. They could not have been prouder of him or more convinced of his altruism than in that moment. Briggs was certainly aware of his life-saving contributions, but would take no credit for them at all. The two men would recount this story throughout the town, which would add to the legend that Doc Briggs had already created and make it that much harder later on for people to believe he could ever have done anything remotely evil.

In the shadows of the empty hospital room, Dr. Oxenbriggs held the tin box of mementos and paced, talking urgently to himself.

"Nick, old boy, you've done it now. Too famous, too brilliant for your own good," he nodded nervously as he walked back and forth in the shadows. "Time to think about moving on, but first, need to best my own record." He stopped, set the box on the desk, and counted on his fingers. "That's it. Need two more patients to send to eternal peace. Who deserves it the most? Let's see." Briggs pulled a list from his lab coat and reviewed it.

"Ah, yes. Frank Robbins. He needs to rest. Too much responsibility on his shoulders. Then, there's Ira West."

Then, Oxenbriggs remembered the television and the reporters coming to town. He knew he needed to be gone. He looked again at his list of names. He paced a moment more, rubbing his head and muttering. Finally, Briggs determined that he would have plenty of time to finish his list of patients after the conference. Oxenbriggs was so lost in his thoughts that he didn't immediately hear his cell phone buzz. Shaken and agitated, Briggs practically growled at the voice on the other end.

"What is it? Oh, thank you for letting me know. I will be right down," he shoved the phone back into his pocket, tucked the box back into its hiding place, and raced out. Oxenbriggs thought this call was the divine message he had been waiting for.

Briggs entered a bright hospital room to find a man of about 55 sitting on the edge of a bed alongside a woman of about the same age. Luvena and Frank Robbins appeared much older than their years, greying and stoop-backed. The years and pains of surviving in the hardscrabble mountains showed on their drooping faces. Yet, they bore a kind of dignity that Briggs had seen for many years both here and back in his hometown.

"Working people," as they called themselves, seemed to survive maladies that would have killed lesser people.

They worked long hours, raised families, and still seemed to always attend all their children's events. No matter what befell them, this group of people, which included Briggs' father and Luvena and Frank Robbins, showed strength and resilience in the face of the most insurmountable adversities. To Briggs, this group of people, more than any other, would appreciate the peace that only death could bring. He would help Frank Robbins, who faced a long life of pain from his ailments, get to peace as quickly as possible. That thought made him smile.

"Frank, Luvena, I am delighted to see you, but I don't think you're so glad to see me," Briggs stood over them, hands on his hips, a broad smile on his face. "What's happening since you were here last? I sent you home to get well."

Admitting they were sick and in need of help came hard to these people. Doc Briggs knew that, so he allowed Frank and Luvena to lead the conversation. He realized the couple suffered a great deal more than health problems. Frank, a former mine laborer, was often without work. He and Luvena's only child, a daughter, got in with a bad crowd in high school and never attended school after she turned sixteen.

By the time she was 18, Marion had one child and was living with a man somewhere in Russell County. Marion never spoke to her parents, seeing their efforts to help her as interference. She drifted farther and farther away. She had become addicted to a variety of pills, or "dope" as the older generation called any variety of addictive drugs. Marion had two more children and was living with yet another man, who was not the father of any of her children. The oldest child, a boy, had started school, and it was there that the county social services office became involved.

Within a year, Marion's children were in the safe and loving arms of their grandparents, Frank and Luvena. Although there was a subsidy from the county, free school lunches, and Medicaid for the children, that didn't cover all the expenses and fees of attending school. When Frank worked, they could just manage. When he had no work, they had to make decisions that some would have considered impossible—whether to go to the doctor for a chest cold or buy winter coats for the children.

That's why Doc Briggs' free community clinic days meant the difference between health and illness to so many of the Franks and Luvenas in the mountains. Luvena had insisted Frank go see about the cough and chest pain that would not relent.

Just a few days later, here he sat in the hospital, bewildered, worried about his future, and hoping that Doc Briggs would bring him good news. Doctor Briggs listened to Frank's rattled breathing, heard his gasps for air, felt his heart pounding. He knew that death would give his beloved patient freedom from pain and peace from all the worry. Suddenly, Briggs realized that Frank was whispering to him.

"Doc." Frank leaned into the doctor. "I am seeing things, hearing things. I never did that before."

"And he yells like crazy sometimes," Luvena added. "The young'uns think he's gone mad because he's always been so peaceful." Luvena looked around to ensure that no one heard them.

Dr. Briggs stared at the pair for a moment. "You are still taking the pills I prescribed? Cannot stop those."

Luvena ignored the question and kept talking about something that Briggs didn't quite follow. "I don't understand. When we came to the community clinic last month, we thought Frank just had a bad chest cold and cough. Nothing like this."

Dr. Briggs recognized that she was questioning his treatment. He had to stop her before she asked too many questions. He smiled. "You're just lucky we found it in time. Pneumonia can kill you." Briggs said softly.

Frank chimed in. "Doc, there's something else," Frank added in his raspy voice. "We ain't got no insurance. I got laid off again."

There was a question that Briggs could answer. "You don't worry about that at all, Frank," Doc Briggs patted Frank's thin arm. "Just do as I tell you, and it will be fine.

You are taking those pills I called in, right?"

Frank nodded. "Doc Briggs. We had to go to Kingsport to get them. The Mutual quit carrying them," Frank said.

"Hmm. Well, how about this," Briggs thought for a moment. "I'll get them for you right here at the hospital."

Luvena talked as if she had not heard the last exchange. She was still bantering on about the hallucinations. "What are you going to do about this crazy talk and yelling?" Luvena pleaded. "Frank's never done that in his life."

Dr. Briggs had to get Luvena to stop. "Just trust me," he said in his most sincere voice. "It's part of the healing process especially with this new medicine. It will settle down soon."

Frank seemed to accept the doctor's response. "Well, I sure hope so. I'm going crazy like this. We're raising our three grandchildren, who are afraid to spend time with me like this," Frank whispered a little louder.

When Luvena spoke again, Briggs realized she had been listening while blabbering. "Doc," Luvena said softly. "We support them kids. So, thank you for working, knowing about our money situation."

Doc Briggs stood up to his full height and looked directly at Luvena. He wanted her to hear and believe his words as if they were a sacred promise. "In a few days, Frank will not be worried about his health at all."

Luvena could not contain her emotions. She stood and

fell, crying into Dr. Briggs' chest. Awkwardly, he wrapped his arms around her and let her cry. A thought occurred to Briggs that perhaps he was helping the wrong member of the family to lasting peace.

"You are a Godsend," Luvena exclaimed as she wiped tears from her eyes. When she realized she had displayed so much emotion to her husband's doctor, Luvena straightened up, stepped backwards, and wiped her tears away with a cloth she had taken from her sweater pocket.

A few days later, Dr. Briggs Oxenbriggs stood in that same hospital room, looking down on a much weaker Frank Robbins, who was struggling to breathe. Helplessly, Frank watched as Doc Briggs, the man he trusted with his life, withdrew a syringe from the breast pocket of his lab coat and in one motion, thrust the contents into a port on Frank's IV.

"Frank, this will take away all your worries," Briggs said as he watched the contents flow through the tube and into Frank's arm.

Still hoping that the doctor was administering some sort of miracle cure, Frank tried to smile and follow the medication. "Oh Doc, I need some help fast. I just want to go home."

"You will go home, my friend. You will go home," Briggs said. Dropping the empty syringe back into his pocket, Briggs watched as the life fought its way out of Frank's body.

He smiled as Frank gasped and convulsed, then fell still and silent. Oxenbriggs straightened the threadbare pajama top Frank wore and ran his fingers down the dead man's right arm, stopping at the Mason ring on Frank's hand. Turning the lifeless hand so that the ring caught the light, Oxenbriggs nodded in admiration. He then slipped the ring off Frank's finger and dropped it into his own jacket pocket.

After a moment, Doctor Oxenbriggs calmly walked out of the room, making certain that no one saw him. After all, he was supposed to be away at a conference. He knew that nurses making their rounds at shift change would find the late Mr. Frank Robbins. Meanwhile, Briggs made his way to the now familiar old wing of the hospital and slipped into the room that had become his sanctuary. Taking his metal box from the nightstand, Briggs opened it. He chose a label, wrote something on it, then tied its string around Frank Robbins' ring. Gently, he placed the piece into the box, closed it, slid it back into the fake drawer opening, and then disappeared into the hallway.

A few hours later, Luvena Robbins sat alone on the edge of the hospital bed, where her husband had been found by nurses making their rounds. Although his body was gone, Luvena could still see the imprint of Frank's head on the pillow and feel the depression of his back in the mattress. She cried openly and wondered why her husband lay dead.

Antibiotics typically cured pneumonia. Luvena was angry at everyone, including God.

She had been raised to believe that He had a plan and nothing happened unless it was for the greater good. But Luvena wondered what could be good about starving some precious children and their grandmother. She looked up at the ceiling.

"I can't believe this, God. You took him from me too soon. All he had was a chest cold," Luvena tried to stop crying just as Ash McKay walked into the room.

"Mrs. Robbins," he said softly. "I'm Dr. McKay. How are you doing?"

"The nurse said I could have a few minutes," she responded.

He told her to take as long as she needed. She said what she had been asking from the beginning of Frank's chest cold, that she couldn't believe he died from a cold. Ash saw an opportunity. He knew what the people here thought of autopsies. They were intrusive and inhuman. The person had suffered and died, so an autopsy seemed to be excessive. Yet, he knew he had to try. Dr. McKay, the man of science, knew an autopsy would answer the question of whether the great Dr. Briggs was deliberately killing his patients. An autopsy would help the Robbins family come to terms with the death of their beloved Frank.

"Mrs. Robbins," Dr. McKay began, "I know this is hard to

think of after all you've been through. But you ought to get an autopsy." He watched her face to see if she was angered by his suggestion. She remained stoic. After a moment, she spoke.

"Cut on him. What good would that do?" Luvena asked. "Where is Doc Briggs? I thought he would be here."

"He left for a medical conference where he's giving the main talk," Dr. McKay maintained his calm tone. "Listen, Mrs. Robbins, an autopsy would answer those questions you have, and who knows, what you learn could help someone else maybe your grandchildren someday."

He stood silent, letting her think about the idea of helping her grandchildren. Finally, she nodded, biting her lip.

"I will get the forms and make the arrangements," Dr. McKay said. "Stay as long as you wish, Mrs. Robbins."

CHAPTER 11

Pressure Plays

As Luvena Robbins was signing the approval form for an autopsy at the hospital, Eliot West sat before a prohibited detective computer and stole a glance around the room to ensure that he was alone. Glancing between the screen and the doorway, he clicked a few keys and anxiously pressed the old computer to spit out the results faster. Eliot tried to control the nervous jitters in his legs. Finally, the results were printing, ever so slowly. West scanned the words. They would reveal whatever secret the great Dr. Oxenbriggs was hiding. First, West wanted to rule out Dr. McKay. He read the search results.

"Ashwood E. McKay. Birth date: January 23, 1981. Birthplace: Utica, New York. License Number: BN.... Well, he's legit. Now for the big man himself," Eliot began typing. Information filled the screen. Eliot read aloud.

"Nicholas W. Oxenbriggs. Birthdate: March 4, 19xx. Birthplace: Brockton, Massachusetts.

Deceased: What?" Eliot exclaimed.

The dates had been obscured. He began to print the

results, then heard voices and footsteps approaching. The mid-morning department meeting had ended. That meant the sheriff and staff would be filling this tiny squad room within seconds. Anxiously, Eliot watched the printer slowly crisscross and jut the page forward. He realized he couldn't clear his search parameters or turn off the computer until the printing finished. Just as the first person, a young file clerk, crossed the threshold into the room, the printer finished. Eliot jerked the page from the printer, wadded it into his jacket pocket, frantically cleared the search, and pressed the computer's off button just as Sheriff Black lumbered into the room, laughing with one of the older deputies. Black threw a hard look at Eliot.

"West. What are you working on?" Sheriff Black demanded.

"That bunch of boys stealing and selling bikes for parts up in East Stone. Looks like we caught a break," Eliot said with as much official calm as he could muster.

"How so?" Black asked mockingly.

West ignored the tone. "Found some kid at the flea market trying to sell bikes but the paint jobs were poor. I had no idea that selling bike parts would make so much money."

Sheriff Black nodded and pushed his wide-brimmed Stetson back on his head. "Around these parts, any money is a lot. I remember the day when we had hardly any crime. It's hard to replace thirty-dollar an hour mining jobs with seven-dollar an hour discount store greeters." The Sheriff realized that the resources he had to use and the caliber of deputy he could hire were directly linked to the taxes that industry paid into the county coffers. He often became frustrated when the new breed of citizen, concerned only about the environment, supported closing manufacturing companies. "And nobody cares. Hell, most people think Virginia ends at Roanoke. They can't even pronounce Appalachia. It's AppleLATCH uh. They say AppleLAY-cha," Sheriff Black was on his soapbox. "We're in the forgotten part of the U.S. of A. In fact, people come here to be forgotten," he said flatly.

"To be forgotten," Eliot had never thought about that until Sheriff Black said it. "People come here to be forgotten," Eliot repeated and realized he had to do some more digging. "Sheriff, you'll have to excuse me. I have to go by the house and check on my dad," Eliot tried to stand up but with the Sheriff's next words, sat back down. Eliot should have known that he could not get anything past the legendary Dove Black, who was pacing angrily in front of Eliot.

"Listen, I know what you're up to," the Sheriff growled. "That crazy notion about Doc Briggs. Have you found the broach? That's what you're supposed to be working on. You were warned, West."

"Sir. I got a tip, and I had to check it out," Eliot tried to say. "And you said I could not investigate without a cause. I have a cause."

Black stopped and towered over him. "What the hell cause do you have to run the licenses and background of two of our doctors? I don't exactly see a charge anywhere? And you are not investigating the missing broach."

"I am working on that–like I said, I got a tip," Eliot tried to sound strong, but facing Black, whose eyes penetrated his soul, Eliot sounded more pleading than confident.

"Just like all those tips you got about illegal stills and pot growing in Tennessee?" Black mocked Eliot.

"This is not the same. It's not fair that you throw that up to me every time you don't like my way of police work," Eliot tried to defend himself, but he could see that Black was only beginning his treatise.

"Your way got you exiled back to here. This is not the big city where cops run license plates and pull reports for recreation," Black said angrily. "I don't give a damn about your hunches and so-called confidential tips. Here, we get to know the community and understand how things are. Unless you can show me hard evidence, you leave the best doctor in this town alone or you can leave your weapon and badge on my desk. Got it?" Black shook his index finger at Eliot, almost as if he were scolding a child.

"Sheriff," Eliot tried to remain calm, confident. "There is something going on."

Sheriff Black ignored him. "The badge and weapon or your word."

Eliot pressed, hoping that if Sheriff Black saw how serious he was, the great man would give him some room to investigate. "If you just let me do my job."

Sheriff Black remained unfazed. "Your job is to find that broach and to check parking and traffic violations and make sure the parks and schools are patrolled. You are not the detective. Now, get out of here before I fire you."

West jumped up and shoved himself out the nearest door that emptied onto Wood Avenue, where he slammed directly into the one person he never wanted to see, Tierney Baynes. She stumbled, nearly losing her balance.

"Hey!" Tierney exclaimed as she gathered her purse and papers before they scattered across the street. Then, Tierney realized the person was her worst enemy, Eliot West. When he looked up to see it was Tierney, he choked off his apology.

"Oh, just what I needed," Eliot stammered.

Tierney turned from surprise to anger. "'Excuse me' is the expected response," she spat out.

"But then, you've never done anything expected, West."

Looking back toward the station, West saw that Sheriff Black was staring out at him. So, he quickly pushed Tierney aside and walked on toward the Mutual. Perhaps if he went in for a cup of coffee, he would be able to shake off the Sheriff's tail, which he knew would be invisible behind him.

After a few blocks, West ducked down a side street and waited for Tierney to pass. As soon as she did, he called her over to him. Perplexed and curious, Tierney made a wide turn, as if she were going to walk toward the card shop on the corner. Eliot had made a snap decision out of desperation, one that he hoped he would not regret. He was going to ask Tierney Baynes for help and take her into his confidence.

"Baynes. Baynes. Look. We need to talk," Eliot said when Tierney was close enough to him.

"Let's admit that we have no love lost between us since Knoxville. But there's something going on here and as much as I hate to say this, I need your help."

Tierney shook her head. "I am not getting involved in some sort of revenge you have."

Eliot knew he had to convince her and get Tierney to trust him. "Tierney, this is about my dad, Doctor Briggs, and that resident, Dr. McKay. Please, listen to me."

Tierney knew that Eliot would never risk his father's life, so she would offer him a few minutes and listen to his pitch. She looked around for a more private place to talk. A few blocks down, construction work was underway on what had been the city's bus station. Built in the 1940's and long since closed, the building, with its curved outer wall of block glass, had been sold again. This time, the new owner planned to restore the building, even opening the original diner inside. Tierney motioned toward the bus station.

"Let's go over there. No one will likely be working on the renovations at the moment," Tierney said. "I'll go first, and then you can meet me there. Go through the back entrance on Fifth Street."

Eliot made his way back toward the Mutual, where once inside, he struggled to appear calm. He bought a cup of coffee and slid into one of the brown, worn, wooden booths to drink it. He pretended to be seriously studying something on his cell phone. He waved hellos to a few people and noticed that several who were there to get prescriptions were leaving empty-handed. Perhaps they couldn't afford the medications.

Perhaps the drug store didn't have their prescription medicines in stock. Whatever the reason, Eliot could not worry about them now. He finished the coffee, carried the cup back to the counter, smiled, said goodbye to the folks behind the counter, and walked slowly out onto Wood Avenue toward the gas station next door and deliberately away from the bus station.

He meandered down Wyadotte, finally ending on Fifth, where he sneaked into the back entrance to the bus station. Construction material dotted the floor space. Shards of light rippled through the glass blocks and spilled across the dusty floor, appearing for all the world like sunlight pieces of quartz.

Looking around to make sure no one else was inside, Eliot spotted Tierney in the farthest corner away from the wall of block glass. He thought that she was at least smart enough to avoid the windows. She was seated on a makeshift bench of two two-by-fours and paint cans. Tierney started talking when she saw Eliot. He put his finger to his lips, motioning her to whisper.

"I'm listening. Want me to retract something?" Tierney mocked.

"I deserve that," Eliot said. "I called you a lot of names back in Knoxville."

"Not to mention running me off the road," Tierney said angrily. "And then having me followed."

"I never did that," Eliot was surprised. "That must have been one of your conspiracies come to life."

Tierney stood to walk off. "Truth or we have nothing to talk about." She gave Eliot a defiant look. He nodded and gestured for her to sit down.

"I never ran anybody off the road there or followed anybody here. Truth," Eliot said. "Another truth. Your story about that doctor and Medicaid fraud made a lot of powerful people mad. More than likely, one of them had you followed," Eliot stared at her.

Tierney considered that idea, contemplated Eliot's straightforward look, and nodded. "Okay, what is going on that you need my help?"

Eliot looked away, thinking. The empty space was silent for a moment. "First, you have to agree to treat me as a confidential source. Nothing I tell you, ask you, show you, or anything will ever be attributed to me," Eliot said flatly.

"Why should I do that? Remember, you're the one in Knoxville who confidentially gave misleading tips to the paper on several stories and made me look like I didn't know how to do my job." Tierney would not let Eliot forget that time.

Eliot reached for his cell phone, thrust it toward Tierney, and flipped through photos until he came to one of him and his dad smiling together. Tierney realized how much Eliot resembled his dad. Tierney studied the photo and then looked at Eliot's face. It was apparent that Eliot West was really doing whatever he was doing to help his dad in some way. But she wasn't ready to trust him completely.

"Do you agree, Baynes, my name out of it?"

"You have my curiosity up. Tell me the topic at least."

"Ah, no. Agree first," Eliot insisted.

Tierney drew a deep breath and thought for a moment. She really wanted to know what was so important to Eliot West that he would stake his father on her trust. She hoped it was something to do with a crime or that doctor who had committed all that Medicaid fraud. But Tierney never dreamed Eliot would be the one to add a piece to the puzzle of the inordinate number of deaths at the hospital. She tried to stay focused and not give in too soon.

"If your story checks out, then I agree," Tierney said.

Eliot was realizing that he had made a mistake in trusting the hair-brained Tierney Baynes. But he had to try one more time. "But what I need is for you to help me check out the information I have. It must be done without involving my name at all."

Tierney saw an opportunity to lecture her adversary. "You walked around in Knoxville the pious police officer above reproach. Everyone trusted you including me."

"Can you come off that? It's so old." Eliot's frustration grew. "I had a wife then. Living in Knoxville on a cop's salary was not easy—especially when she got sick."

Tierney's self-righteousness dripped through her next words. "So, you stole from the criminals and sold to the criminals. Then arrested them again."

Eliot was really mad and impatient. He could have kicked himself for believing he could trust this so-called reporter. He spewed out his anger toward her. "You, the great investigative reporter, caught me. My wife recovered and divorced me. You should be happy."

"Well, I know only one person who will be happy to know you're single," Tierney responded in a lyrical, sweet tone.

Eliot was confused. He wondered what in the world Tierney was talking about. She certainly didn't answer his question or even respond to his accusations toward her. She was completely off-topic. Eliot would not let Tierney distract him. "Can we just agree to hate each other forever? Right now, there's something more important," Eliot growled, studying Tierney's face. He was ready to walk away. "Aw, hell. Why did I think "

Tierney realized she had pushed too far, and she really wanted to know what tantalizing story Eliot West possessed. "Hey! All right. All right," Tierney jumped to her feet and tugged at Eliot's shirtsleeve. "You would not have come to me if you had any other way. You have my word that I will tell no one."

Eliot turned and studied her face. "Neither of us wants anyone to die unnecessarily."

That red-flag word caught Tierney's full attention. "Die unnecessarily? What is this"

Eliot cut her off. "And we agree that if we can stop someone from dying, we will."

"You are not making sense," Now, it was Tierney's turn to be confused by Eliot's response.

Pacing across the dusty floor, in and out of the shards of sunlight, Eliot huffed, crossed his arms, rubbed his head, and nodded as if he were having an internal argument. "Ok, here goes. This is going to sound crazy, but the highly-respected Dr. Nicholas W. Oxenbriggs is deliberately giving patients the wrong medicine "

Tierney exclaimed over him. "Briggs? But it's McKay who has always been in the room and signed the death certificates."

"Wait! What do you know?" Eliot was astonished that Tierney knew something about the situation at the hospital.

Tierney realized she had given away too much. She tried to back track. "Uh, nothing. I just talk to a lot of families in writing my obits," Tierney tried to cover her eagerness.

Eliot needed to know what Tierney was hiding. "But it's Oxenbriggs who is prescribing a medication for my father that causes serious side effects."

Tierney tried hard to remember her reporter demeanor. Don't be too eager, and don't jump to conclusions. "Lots of medicines cause side effects different for each patient. What's the news in that?"

Eliot's response told Tierney that she was on the right track. In fact, she nearly jumped off the two-by-four seat. "This one causes hallucinations, violent outbursts, and even death," Eliot said.

Eliot noticed that Tierney stiffened. "If you know this, then why is he not under arrest, Eliot?"

The words toppled out, and Eliot felt he could not control what he was saying. "The medication is called Haldol. It's for schizophrenia. My father is not schizophrenic. Dr.

Oxenbriggs has given him that medication."

Still trying to be a journalist, Tierney forced herself to remain calm. "Why would Dr. Oxenbriggs give a medicine like that to your father?"

"That's what I want to know," Eliot said. "He suffered from hallucinations and weird dreams. Hell, he improved when that student doctor at the hospital treated him."

Tierney tried to cover her excitement and confusion. She was sure the person responsible for the deaths was Dr. McKay because he had either been the last person to see the victim alive or he had signed the death certificates. As far as Tierney had been able to determine, Briggs had not been directly linked to any of the deaths. She tried to hide her keen interest and mental calculations.

"You mean Dr. McKay?" Tierney questioned.

"How did yes. He treated my father."

"Okay. So, Dr. Oxenbriggs gave your father the wrong medicine?" Tierney really hoped that Eliot would say that the police had launched an investigation. That would make Will Hutton take her seriously. She pushed Eliot for more. "That's medical malpractice, but are the police investigating?"

Eliot was so frustrated with Tierney. She didn't listen too carefully. "But didn't you hear me? What I suspect is that the great Dr. Oxenbriggs has prescribed that medication for more than just my father."

"Then," Tierney insisted, "you're a cop, a trained investigator. Why don't you just do your job? You have access to more information at your fingertips than I have." She watched Eliot's face.

He bit his lip and hesitated. "I cannot simply go around investigating private citizens without cause."

Then, Tierney knew. Sheriff Dove Black had somehow caught Eliot trying to investigate and put a stop to it. "So, you've gotten your wings clipped already. That's why you've come to me. That's why you slammed into me outside the police station just now. You'd come from getting caught."

Eliot nodded sheepishly. "And there's more. This is the strangest part of all. I'm not sure Oxenbriggs is really his name."

Tierney's placid, controlled look suddenly disappeared. She leaned forward, eager. Perplexed. The silence worked. Eliot filled it with words that raced out.

"I found a partial birth record. If he is Oxenbriggs, he could be 80 years old. But it could be a misprint. I didn't have time to confirm it, and the printer was not working well."

Tierney would not let him off that easily. "You mean you were caught before you could get the full details," Tierney said triumphantly. "Why won't the Sheriff let you investigate?"

"Does Will Hutton let you follow every hunch you get?"

Eliot spat back at her.

Tierney recalled her last conversation with Will. He had threatened to fire her for her mere suspicions of wrong-doing and death. She realized she and Eliot could help each other.

"Okay. What makes you think the doctor changed his name?" Tierney asked skeptically.

"He is not 80 years old, for one thing. The letters were smeared, so I couldn't read the year, but it appears to make Oxenbriggs much older. Listen, I'll get you what I found."

Tierney still wasn't sure whether she should trust Eliot. "If this is some sort of sick revenge, West..."

"I don't play games with my daddy's life. And right now, I'm his insurance policy. Just check out what I've told you."

She studied Eliot as she recalled the stories she had heard of others who had suffered hallucinations, violent outbursts, and untimely deaths. Now, Eliot was telling her similar information, like another piece of the puzzle. "Give me whatever you have on paper, but don't send it to the office."

"You know the rock pillar at the entrance to Bullitt Park? There's a loose rock–third from the top on the right. I'll put one of the Welcome Tickets in it. No phone calls, no e-mails, no texts. No contact," Eliot instructed. "Get me the information tonight. You have that database in the newsroom."

Tierney realized she would have to find a way to access the database because there would not be time to go to the library and get her stories done in time. In fact, this meeting with Eliot had cost her nearly an hour—one she would have to find a way to hide from Will.

Tierney shook her head. That's when Eliot realized she was on a short leash as well.

"Ah, I see," he gave her a wry smile. "Same boat as me. Fired if you investigate. Well, that's some justice. Listen, we cannot have any connection for both our sakes. You better keep my name out of this."

Tierney replied in a smooth tone. "Out of what? There's nothing here."

Eliot pulled out his cell phone and looked at the time. "I have to go. When you get something, just leave it back in the rock crevice. I will check there in the morning."

"First, I'll figure out if you're lying," Tierney warned.

Later that night in the newsroom, Tierney checked to make certain she was alone before she slid open the envelope that she had retrieved from behind the rock at the entrance to Bullitt Park. Hurriedly, Tierney sat down at her desk and began punching keys on her laptop.

She whispered to herself. "If you are NOT him, who are you, and how do I find out? This could take forever," Tierney complained in a whisper. She was startled by the booming voice behind her. Will Hutton had come in, and Tierney was so lost in her searching that she had not heard him come in from the pressroom.

"Where have you been, and what are you doing?" Will demanded. "Obits don't write themselves."

"Shit!" Tierney jumped "Will! You scared me. I'm following a lead on the missing broach." Tierney lied.

Will leaned in to glance at her computer screen. "In the Massachusetts birth records database? And how much is that costing us?" Will stated coldly. "I've a good mind to fire you right here." He glared at her.

Undeterred, Tierney pressed Will. "Can we talk so that the entire newsroom doesn't hear? Please, Will," Tierney held up a hand. "And before you ask, all my obits are in your bin. None at the front desk either. Profile to bed as well."

Will held out his hand, motioning for the piece of paper on Tierney's desk. Reluctantly, she handed it over. "I dread asking. But how did you get this, and what's it supposed to mean?"

"It is the birth record for Dr. Nicholas Oxenbriggs," Tierney offered eagerly. "But it's garbled. It didn't print correctly."

"And how did you come by it? And don't say anonymous tip," Will demanded. "Tierney, there's no way to tell if this piece of paper is authentic or just something someone printed and faked, or whether there is more than one

Oxenbriggs." He pushed it back at her. "Nothing ties this to our doctor."

"That's why I was looking for his medical license and to see if there are any photos anywhere," Tierney explained.

"You can't trace the chain of custody or anything." Will shook his head. Then, he abruptly changed course. "Are there photos of our Doc Briggs? Awh! I'm going to hate this, but if your stories are in, there's nothing new on the broach, and you're set up for tomorrow, take the evening and look it up—but only one search of the databases. They are too expensive."

Tierney jumped on his instruction. "But where do I start since I don't know if our Doctor was someone else before?"

"How about you start with our Doc's university and med school credentials," Will offered. "See if they have a yearbook or anything with a photo. You could also call his last employer—but they've likely closed for the night."

Tierney hurriedly sat down at her desk and began flipping through papers and searching for information on the computer. After a few moments, she rose and walked into Will's office. Tierney knew he might order her off the investigation, but she had to take a chance. There was little she could do. Given the late hour, most offices she needed to call were closed. Standing in Will's doorway, she watched for a moment as he ran his hand through his dark shock of rich, black hair. He reminded her of a famous actor, dark hair, blue eyes, and in constant motion, but deliberate and thoughtful. She spoke softly.

"Will, I am getting nowhere because the offices are closed." She was not going to ask for permission to continue tomorrow. "I'll have to make those calls in the morning. But how about the drug? Why can't I trace the families who've reported weird things with the victims—their loved ones who died? I could call some of them tonight."

For once, Will spoke kindly, softly. "That's not documentation, T. It's still supposition, and we don't do that here. You are not calling any families. No need to upset them—if you're wrong. It would be terrible if the facts got in the way of a good story."

Then, Tierney remembered her notebook. She took a chance. "Will, I don't have to call them." She rushed back to her desk, grabbed the well-worn reporter's notebooks, and then rushed back into Will's office, where she dropped them triumphantly onto his desk.

He shook his head. "Dare I ask?"

Tierney tried to talk calmly, but struggled. "I've been keeping notes of all the deaths, and they are matched to those in which families reported uncharacteristic behavior and those who reported a medication." She watched Will, who now held his head propped in both hands. "Will, there have been 29 in total in the six months—and I did what you said and looked back as far as I could go. However, since no one thought this was odd, no one kept records until I came here."

"Tierney, none of this rises to the level of a news story," Will closed the notebooks and handed them back to her. "There's nothing here."

"Will—can I have time tomorrow to follow up?" Tierney realized the moment she asked the question, she should not have done so.

"No," Will turned his attention to his computer, but glanced up at Tierney and let out a tired sigh. "Hell, stories first. No contact with anyone local—I mean anyone."

In the newsroom the next morning, Tierney Baynes was working the phone when people began arriving. She had already called Briggs' last hospital and gotten less than nothing from the human resources department. All they would provide were the dates of his employment. She learned he had been there for ten years and one month, but nothing more. In fact, the representative clammed up when Tierney asked about the great doctor's performance, or even problems. Tierney thought that was suspicious. When Will arrived, closely followed by Emily, Tierney didn't let him get to his desk before she started peppering him with questions and her suspicions. Will was not amused, much less interested.

"I don't want to know," Will said sardonically. "Wait—another conspiracy—no even better—a hunch. By the way, don't you sleep?"

Will Hutton threw out his arms–mocking her. As he started to respond, his phone buzzed, and he grabbed it, answered, looked surprised, and hung up. Tierney and Emily had listened intently, then gestured to one another that they couldn't hear anything.

So much for all your "investigative" work, T. They've just brought in Ash McKay for the theft of that broach. Now, you have a story. Emily, take the lead on this. T- get your obits done and you can help her. Start at the Sheriff's office, and T, once you're done, get to the hospital for a statement. I'll send a photographer. Glad I came in early."

Emily and Tierney grabbed their notebooks and raced out.

At about the same time Tierney was asking questions of Dr. Oxenbriggs' former employer, the great man had returned from his medical conference and secreted himself in the abandoned room in the unused hospital wing. He was carefully studying patients' charges and making notes. He was astonished to see that several of his patients had been discharged, and apparently, he had approved the discharge orders. He wasn't certain how that had happened. Dr. Briggs was counting on several of those patients to help him meet his goal. Briggs grabbed the charts and headed for a nurses' station, where he stopped a passing nurse.

"So, all these patients were discharged while I was away?" Dr. Briggs asked.

"Why yes," the nurse responded with a friendly smile. "You know, we were hoping you'd be here for those TV people who did the story on the RAM. They wanted to interview you," the nurse said, moving to a computer screen and bringing up the patient charts.

"And you followed all my orders even the ones I called in?" Briggs asked. "Where are those?"

The nurse punched a few keys on the keyboard and showed Dr. Oxenbriggs his orders for the patients.

"See. They are right here. Exactly as you dictated."

Oxenbriggs studied the screen and thought for a moment. "McKay," he said flatly.

"Shall I page Dr. McKay?" the nurse asked.

"Uh, no thank you," Briggs responded. "I will take care of it."

CHAPTER 12
The Noose

Sheriff Dove Black calmly guided a visibly shaking Ash McKay into the squad room and motioned for him to sit down in an empty chair near one of the desks. McKay was not handcuffed, but his face showed the fear of a caged animal that had a gun pointed at its head. He quietly complied. Still in his lab coat, McKay struggled to control tears, wiping them with the collar of his jacket. He wondered why the sheriff was taking so long to sit down and caught himself following the lumbering man as he opened and closed file drawers, taking out papers, examining them, and then putting them back. After repeating these actions several times and beginning a soft hum, Black held up one page, read it carefully, then stopped humming. In one surprisingly graceful move, the sheriff turned to McKay, stopped humming, and slid silently into a chair across from the doctor.

"Dr. McKay, you don't have to talk to me," Sheriff Black said calmly.

Ash swallowed hard and gulped in a deep breath of air.

"I know, Sheriff, but I don't know how that broach got onto my desk. Anyone could have placed it there."

Black never looked at McKay, staring instead at the paper in front of him. Ash could see it was some sort of standard form. "I see," Sheriff Black retained his soft, calm tone. "It's worth a lot of money—could be a nice windfall for a doctor with massive student debt." Black never looked up.

Ash shook his head and tried to stop his knees from quivering. "But that's not something I would do, or even think about doing," he said emphatically.

A movement near the front entrance to the squad room caught Ash's attention. Eliot West sort of sauntered in. When he saw that Ash McKay was being questioned by Sheriff Black, Eliot could not hide his shocked look. So, he tried to walk calmly toward them. Ash saw Eliot as the validation for his claim that he did not steal anything, including that ruby broach. So, he sat up straighter.

"Eliot, tell him," Ash blurted out.

"I can't tell him anything, Dr. McKay," Eliot was obviously chagrined. "I trusted you with my father, with my family." Eliot stood near the end of the table, between both men.

Sheriff Black spoke up then. "West, you need to step away since you have a personal connection."

"It's not like that, Sheriff," Eliot looked directly at Sheriff Black, whose stare could have frightened someone other than Eliot.

Before Eliot could speak, Ash began a long chain of pleas. “I didn’t take that broach, and it doesn’t make sense that a thief would just leave that piece out in the open—after all this time—for someone to find. Please, Sheriff Black. You have to believe—”

“Not just someone. A nurse found it—right there on your desk,” Sheriff Black finally looked at Ash, who withered beneath the cold stare.

Ash gulped and pleaded with Eliot to tell the sheriff what the pair had been discussing. However, Eliot shook his head and gave Ash an angry look. “That was all obviously a cover,” Eliot said.

Sheriff Black shoved back his chair and bolted up. “What the hell is going on, and does it have anything to do with all those clandestine meetings you two have had over the last few weeks?”

“Eliot, I thought you were investigating,” Ash said, stricken.

“Shut the hell up,” Eliot growled at Ash and just wished he had never met the doctor. “I don’t know what to think now.”

Sheriff Black stepped into Eliot’s space, so close that he could feel the sheriff breathing. “West, you mean to tell me you’ve been investigating on the side—and something this guy told you?”

"No. Sir! That's the point. He came to me with a crazy story about Dr. Oxenbriggs," Eliot said angrily. "I never once did anything about it."

"Even that day you ran Doc Briggs through the records system?" Sheriff Black didn't budge.

"I do know what goes on in my department. But now, West, you'd better start explaining why."

Eliot stepped back, turning away from Sheriff Black, and began pacing the area around the table. "I found this drug in my dad's hospital chart–one I thought was out of place. Doc Briggs had prescribed it. I asked McKay here why. At first, he defended Oxenbriggs, then finally broke down and told me. We met..."

Sheriff Black cut him off. "West, McKay, you two are in over your head. At the least, it's conspiracy. At the most, it's grand theft. That broach is worth more than 500 dollars."

Ash McKay thought he had nothing more to lose now. His career was gone. He would be in debt forever if he ever got out of jail, and all those patients, including Ira West, were doomed. He had come to Southwest Virginia with such high expectations, and he would be leaving in despair and disgrace. He remembered that night, years ago, when he had had dinner with the incomparable Dr. Oxenbriggs. He was so charming, so confident, and everyone loved him.

Leaving behind cardiology was the right decision back then. That decision had led to this new, unrelenting hell.

Surrounded by two police officers and the suspicions that smothered him, Ash was no longer afraid. If he was going to spend the rest of his life behind bars, Ash McKay would go there knowing he had fought hard for the truth, for his patients, and for himself.

"Sheriff, if you know everything that goes on, then you know that Dr. Oxenbriggs has a secret stash of items collected from deceased patients. He keeps them in an empty room on the unused wing of the hospital. It's creepy," McKay looked the sheriff in the eye when he spoke. The fear had turned into hard resolve.

Sheriff Black stood stoically, unemotional. Ash could not tell whether his statement and change in attitude had made an impact or not.

Then, Sheriff Black spoke softly, purposely, "Very credible coming from the man caught with a dead patient's valuable jewelry. Who's to say you didn't steal from patients and then turn the suspicion on Doc Briggs? He's been here over a decade without a hint of trouble," Black stared at McKay.

Ash played his next card. "And then there's the question of the medication—Haldol. It's for people who suffer from schizophrenia," he said with such dead calm that he knew the sheriff would believe him now. "He's routinely prescribing it for people who don't have the disease. I found that in more than a half-dozen patients. Eliot's father was one of them. But if he goes to see Briggs anymore, he could be the next victim."

Accustomed to reading the unspoken language of a patient's body, Ash knew he had struck a chord with Sheriff Black. The great man blinked quickly and pursed his lips and squinted. "Victim? Of what? Doc Briggs would not hurt his patients." It was a statement, not a question.

Ash wanted the sheriff to understand how much he wanted to be wrong about Dr. Oxenbriggs. For without Briggs, Ash could not finish his program. He could not become a community physician or any other kind. In fact, Ash McKay had invested everything he had—his future, his talents, and all the student loans he would ever receive—on the reputation of "Briggs" Oxenbriggs. Ash faced Sheriff Black.

"I did not believe it at first. However, I am a scientist and researcher, so I began to do my own research. I found at least 35 patients, so far, this year that had been prescribed the drug without any presenting symptoms. I told Eliot, but he didn't believe me either."

Black studied McKay in silence. If he was lying, McKay was doing a damn good job, Sheriff Black thought. He, too, had observed people throughout his career. They lied by stuttering, by looking away, by staring you down, but something about McKay's demeanor and desperation told Sheriff Black to give the young doctor the benefit of the doubt. The Sheriff started to speak, when Emily Scott breezed into the squad room. The Sheriff did not want to talk with her—especially since the little ditz always introduced herself as if they had never met. He knew it was all an act. She was as shrewd and calculating as he was. For that, Black admired the girl. But her presence never meant good news. She marched right up to him, and as she always did, Emily Scott introduced herself.

"Hi, Sheriff. I'm Emily Scott with the Daily Star," Emily said warmly.

"I know who you are, Ms. Scott, and you know I cannot talk to you now," Sheriff Black said sweetly.

"I understand you've arrested Dr. Ash McKay for the theft of the ruby broach?" Emily continued in her lyrical voice.

Ash McKay and Eliot both looked toward Emily. They were jointly surprised at how fast she had gotten that information, even though it was mostly incorrect. In fact, Emily's statement frightened Ash McKay because as far as he knew, he had not been charged with anything.

She prattled on. "You did make the arrest?"

Emily looked around the sheriff, who had blocked the table. She saw Eliot, and her heart fluttered. After all these years, he was still the best-looking man she had ever seen. Emily didn't seem to care that Eliot did not share her feelings. Sheriff Black was saying something about more information by four o' clock.

"Hi Eliot," Emily said sweetly. "It's good to see you."

Eliot didn't look at her but offered a wave that simultaneously said hello and get lost. However, the man across the table from Eliot started to stand. Sheriff Black wheeled around and shoved the man back into the chair. Undeterred, the man spoke in a rush, ignoring the Sheriff's glare.

"Ms. Scott, wait. I'm Dr. Ash McKay," he said.

"Dr. McKay, tell me about the charges against you," Emily asked. She knew she would not have much time.

Sheriff Black ordered her to leave. "Ms. Scott, I am in the middle of interviewing Dr. McKay."

"I didn't steal that broach, Ms. Scott. I didn't," Ash McKay struggled to see Emily as the sheriff tried to block him.

"What do you know about the theft?" Emily pressed.

By now, Sheriff Black had put a strong hand on Ash's shoulder and squeezed. Ash knew this was his only chance at saving any of his patients.

"I am not the one everyone should be looking at," Ash persisted. "Patients are in danger."

"Wait. What did you say? Is that a threat to patients?" Emily questioned.

Sheriff Black did not want this to get out of hand. He could easily see these rumors turning into hysteria. He had to squash all this right now. "No patients or anyone else is in danger. Now, Ms. Scott, will you please let me finish my work here?"

Sheriff Black planted himself directly between Ash

McKay and Emily Scott and motioned for her to leave. She stared at the sheriff for a moment, then turned.

"Well, there are other folks I can speak with," Emily said lightly, but the sheriff knew it was a threat. Before he could speak, Eliot West's cell phone buzzed. He opened it, listened for a moment, and then turned to the Sheriff.

"Uh, Sheriff. It's my mother—well it's really my dad. They are at the hospital," Eliot seemed to be torn as to whether he should stay or go. Sheriff Black was about to tell him to leave, but Ash McKay spoke first.

"Eliot, you must get him to go to Kingsport. I warned you," Ash pleaded. "He's getting weaker, and this time could be fatal," Ash turned to Black. "Sheriff, you must let me go help," Ash begged.

As Eliot raced out of the squad room, he could hear Ash McKay yelling. "Eliot, Eliot, get your dad out of that hospital. There's no time. Take him to the ER in Kingsport."

Eliot ran to his motorcycle, shoved on his helmet, and took off toward Lone Mountain Medical Center on the east side of town. Over the last few months, this old Harley, the wind in his face, and the winding mountain roads had been Eliot's therapy. He worked out all his problems, made decisions, and cast off anger and frustration. He knew the back roads, the roads through once-proud coal camps, with names like Derby, Imboden, Exeter, Roda and Stonega. He had friends in Keokee, and they often met there and rode into Harlan County, Kentucky.

Eliot knew that the rest of the world either thought this area didn't exist, or if they did know about it at all, they imagined that the residents were toothless hillbillies wearing bibbed overalls. Eliot knew better. These were the hardest working, most generous people he knew. Most went to training beyond high school, and he hadn't seen anyone wearing a pair of bibbed overalls in his lifetime. Certainly, there were drugs, alcoholism, illegal pot farms, and crimes.

The area also experienced the worst unemployment in the entire Commonwealth. There were just no real jobs. Because of the high unemployment, service agencies could not meet the demand for services. People struggled, and many died young because they could not afford medical care. Organizations like RAM and the Health Wagon did the best they could to provide healthcare, but both needed more resources, more medicine, more staff, more money.

That's why Dr. Oxenbriggs had been such a God-send. He had stayed. He had taken the model created by RAM and institutionalized it. Now, residents in all fields rotated in and out of the clinics and medical centers here, and even as far away as Kingsport, Eliot was certain that people had lived and led better lives because of that work. So, he asked himself, why would a guy who does that want to harm his patients? It didn't make any sense at all. No one else had ever reported anything negative about Oxenbriggs.

However, why would Ash McKay seem so desperate to get Ira West out from Oxenbriggs' care? Ash had said "patients" and "lives." Apparently, he thought more people were at risk. Had McKay talked to other families? Had he made these wild charges to anyone else? But there was one thing that made Eliot believe Ash McKay—his father's improvement when Dr. Oxenbriggs was away for a week. That had to mean something. Perhaps it meant that Ash McKay was telling the truth. After all, Eliot himself had questioned the medication his dad was prescribed. He could not take any chances with his father's life. As far as he could see, there was no negative outcome in following Ash McKay's warning.

At the hospital, Eliot entered his father's hospital room to find Ira alternatively pacing the floor and then resting on the edge of the bed. Ira was dressed in his pants, socks, and tee-shirt and had one of those cotton hospital gowns draped over him. It floated loosely as Ira paced.

"Son, your mother insisted that I see Dr. Oxenbriggs," Ira complained. "He got back to town, and she wouldn't rest until she had an appointment."

Ira added that he had been improving, no weird dreams, no pains, no outbursts. "But I had a tiny heart flutter this morning and made the mistake of telling your mother," Ira growled. "I'm only doing this for her, you know. I'm fine."

Ira and Etta West met in college at the University of

Virginia. He had come to school on a track scholarship because he had been a star runner at Rye Cove High School. Etta was studying art history and had plans to teach someday. Etta's mother had described the couple as "two people from opposite sides of the brain." Ira was analytical and deliberate. Etta displayed a creative streak so bold that it manifested itself in her mother's flower garden. She painted the ground with impressionistic images concocted of flowers. Etta and her family had lived in Keokee for generations. One look into her deep, brown eyes and Ira West was what he called "a goner." He lived to make her happy, to see her smile, and to breathe in her sunlight.

For her part, Etta knew Ira cherished her, and that made her love him even more. Her friends at college said Ira was a bit on the "geeky side." But Etta thought he was cute and funny. She liked that he was independent, analytical, and helped her stay with a project until it was finished. Ira West seemed, for all the world, to be an affable, low-key gentleman, always happy to go along with the crowd and not too concerned about his own opinions. He wore an impish smile most of the time, giving the impression that he had a secret just waiting to be told. Beneath that genteel exterior, Ira West calculated each movement. He could analyze and "read people", knowing long before others the true nature of a man or woman. Eliot wished he could gain his father's ability, but perhaps it took all of Ira's years in forensic accounting to develop that skill. But his dad was not seeing Dr. Oxenbriggs clearly.

Etta breezed into the room, carrying a duffle bag, her purse, and a book. Eliot rushed over to take the items from her and set them next to the recliner. Apparently, she had heard Ira complaining.

"You two! I called, and Doc Briggs himself took the call. Said I'd better bring him on in. A doctor in Kingsport is good for filling in, but there's no one like Dr. Oxenbriggs. He's already been in once—fussed at us for even thinking of leaving him. He actually seemed hurt," Etta chided.

In that moment, Eliot realized with all certainty that McKay was telling the truth. He had to do something.

"Mama. Please. Listen to me. You don't need Dr. Oxenbriggs. Daddy, tell her what you really want," Eliot appealed to his father.

"Son, I've tried," Ira said as he plopped onto the bed. Eliot walked to him. Ira whispered. "But she sat and cried and worried. I can't stand to see her cry, son. I just can't."

Etta walked to the bed and began to motion for Ira to swing his feet onto the mattress as she covered him. "Ira," she chided. "You should not tell our boy that."

"Etta, he is a grown man. He's a police officer. I think he can handle this," Ira sounded defiant.

Eliot had to ask about the Haldol. He hoped his mother had not gone to the Mutual and gotten a new prescription, but knew he would be wrong. "Mama, I don't mean to be disrespectful, but I know you. You went right to the Mutual drugstore when Daddy got out of here last week. Now, let me see the pills. I know you have them."

Etta left Ira's bed, made her way slowly across the tiny room, pulled a brown pill bottle from her purse, and handed to Eliot, who had followed her. In turn, he marched back to his father's bed and held out the bottle.

"Daddy, this is the stuff that's giving you the weird dreams and making you see things. Do NOT take it,'" Eliot pleaded.

Etta's voice gave away her anger. "Despite what you say and how they questioned me at the Mutual, Doc Oxenbriggs says it will keep him from having that swallowing trouble." She had stomped back to the bed to plant herself on the opposite side. She stared at Eliot, but he was undeterred.

"Daddy. Are you schizophrenic?" Eliot asked flatly.

"I am not mentally ill," Ira said defiantly.

"That's the point," Eliot pressed forward on his point. "This medicine is for people who ARE."

Etta's temper flared. "Where did you go to medical school?" she demanded.

Eliot tried to ignore her because he had realized his father's life was at stake. "I looked this up. It's called Haldol. In schizophrenics, it helps. But in people like Daddy without the disease, Haldol causes psychotic episodes, violent outbursts, and even death. Please don't take it," Eliot begged.

His mother was astonished and angry and scared. "Dr. Oxenbriggs knows what he's doing. He loves your daddy," Etta said.

Eliot looked at his mother. Her eyes welled with tears, and she looked so alone. He had gone too far. Now, he would likely get no support.

"Mamma, I love daddy, too," Eliot reached to touch his mother's arm, but she jerked away. "I don't know yet why Dr. Oxenbriggs is giving daddy this medicine. But think for a minute. He's gotten better when he's not been taking it," Eliot turned to his father. "Daddy, please help."

For a moment, the room was silent, and then Ira spoke soft and lovingly. "Etta, honey. Give the boy a chance here. He is right. I do feel better without that medicine."

Etta nervously paced the room, rubbing her head. Then she stopped, studying the faces of her husband and then her son. She walked to the bed and took Ira's hand into hers.

"I want what will make you better, Ira. Dr. Oxenbriggs has always been there for us," Etta said in a shaking, soft voice. She nodded.

"I promise if I feel the least bit like my throat is closing up," Ira said, "I'll take the pill."

Etta drew a long, tired breath. "All right. But only for the weekend. If you are still having spells on Monday, it's right back here," Etta said.

Eliot wasted no time. He didn't want to give his mother a chance to change her mind. "Okay. Now, let me get you out of here. I'll drive you to Kingsport right now," Eliot said quickly. He moved to get his father's coat and then to the bed, where he began to help his dad remove the hospital gown.

Etta walked to the bed, shaking her head. "But we're waiting on Doc Briggs to come back. We can't just leave," she stated emphatically.

"Yes, we can. Come on. Hurry," Eliot urged, grabbing his father's jacket. He didn't wait for Ira to remove the hospital gown. He hustled his parents to the door, where to his despair, Dr. "Briggs" Oxenbriggs opened the door and pushed the trio back inside. He greeted them with a wide, friendly smile.

"Whoops!" Briggs exclaimed. "Not thinking of leaving me, Ira? We have to get you well first," Briggs said.

Ira stood still in the middle of the room and protested. "I'm feeling 100 percent, and there's no sense spending money and time on a healthy man. Save this room for someone who needs it."

Briggs patted Ira on the shoulder. "Let me be the judge of that."

"Dr. Oxenbriggs, I think my dad is right," Eliot grabbed his father's arm and tried to lead him around Dr. Oxenbriggs.

Etta took a couple of steps to stand facing Eliot. "We must listen to Doc Briggs, Eliot," Etta said.

Briggs used the opportunity to begin slowly walking Ira back to the bed. "Now, Ira. You need rest. All this strain is taking its toll. You just lie down, and I'll send in a nurse to help you while I go order some tests," Briggs finished and watched as Ira lay down on the bed.

"Dr. Briggs, I have some questions. May I come with you?" Etta asked.

Dr. Oxenbriggs studied her for a moment and held out an arm. She took it with a smile and left the room. Once they were out of earshot, Eliot pleaded with his father.

"You need to do something," Eliot begged. "You need to fire Dr. Oxenbriggs and change doctors."

"But son. You can't fire a doctor," Ira said flatly.

Eliot refused to give up. "Like I've said, go to Kingsport just to the hospital there. Check yourself in."

Ira raised up on the bed. "And tell them what? We don't have records, and they will ask for them."

"Look, Daddy. We need to get you out of here," Eliot began to pace. "You do well when Doc Briggs is off on one of his two or three day conferences. Then, you get worse when he comes back."

"Okay. If you will hush, I'll go," Ira nodded. "But what

about Mother?" Ira gestured toward the door.

"What about her?" Eliot asked.

"It will give her a stroke going against Doc Oxenbriggs," Ira explained. "She thinks he's a god."

"Daddy," Eliot urged. "The point is that you need to get where you can get real help."

"She will be back any moment," Ira gestured toward the door. "Don't say a word. I'll talk to her." He lay down and covered up on the bed.

"Dad. I left in such a hurry that I parked my bike in the emergency lot," Eliot said frantically. "They will tow me. Where's your car? I will need that to get us to Kingsport," Eliot asked.

Ira thought for a moment. "Son, mother parked in the lot at the back, in the second row. She kept the keys, unfortunately," Ira said. "No, wait. There's her purse." Ira pointed to a brown, leather purse near the recliner.

Eliot grabbed the keys and hurried out of the room. Meanwhile, Dr. Briggs had listened to Etta West, who had been concerned that Eliot took those pills Dr. Briggs said Ira could not live without. Dr. Briggs patted her arm and assured her he had things well in hand. He urged her to go back and stay with Ira.

In his darkened, unused hospital room, Dr. Oxenbriggs paced, talking to himself and packing a duffle bag with his mementos. He pulled a passport from a box that held several.

"Damn! Damn! Damn! Nick, old man. This is it," Briggs paced and randomly grabbed things from the room. "You would have to pick a cop's dad. Almost as bad as St. Louis, where it was a priest. That was close. But you're a sly one. Luckily, no one really checks references too deeply."

"Employers are afraid of lawsuits, so they don't share negative information. Name, dates of employment, and job titles. Easy. A few fake references. I'll hand in my resignation on Monday and be gone as soon as I can. Just let me help my patient, Ira West, to peace, and no loose ends." Briggs smiled at the cleverness of his plan.

Looking down the hallway to ensure that no one saw him, Oxenbriggs left the room and headed out of the hospital with his bag full.

In the late sun reflecting off the metal desks inside the Daily Star newsroom, Emily Scott looked at the clock and wrote faster. She quickly checked her notes, then typed furiously, clicking the computer keys as she muttered to herself. Emily briefly acknowledged Tierney as she breezed into the newsroom. She fell into the chair at her desk, opened the computer, and began to write. Emily finished her story, triumphantly pressed the "send" button, then fell back against the back of her chair.

"Sheriff Black had Ash McKay right in front of me," Emily complained. "I tried to talk to him. He said he didn't do anything wrong, and then he said something weird."

Tierney chimed in. "Hospital won't talk. Said it's a police matter," Tierney said mockingly.

"I did manage to get a nurse coming off duty to tell me a little. She said another nurse found the broach when Dr. McKay sent her to get his phone, which he left on his desk. The broach was under it," Tierney stopped to breathe. Then, she realized something that Emily had said. "Wait, something weird?"

"Yeah," Emily said. "He said patients were in danger."

Will Hutton stomped into the newsroom and gave them skeptical looks.

"Listen up," Will offered advice. "I have never met a guilty convict. Sounds like the former Doctor McKay had more plans and was luckily caught before he could realize them."

Emily shook her head. "You think so? Will, I got an entirely different impression."

Will admonished her. "You haven't been around long enough, Emily," he said, then turned to Tierney. "And you are not prone to conspiracy theories."

"Will, I was right all along," Tierney said emphatically. "Something has been going on at the hospital."

Will towered over her. "A theft of a broach, no matter how valuable, is not murder," Will cautioned. "And Doc Briggs, whom you suspected, is not an identity thief. Do you have anything of value–anything we can confirm?

When you were at the hospital, did you talk to Briggs?"

Tierney shook her head. "They paged him several times, but he didn't respond."

Will stood and thought, then said, "He has a house and a truck—I think it's a Ford pick-up. See if he's at home."

"I'm on it. Let me finish these obits," Tierney said.

"Nope," Will said. "I'm still in charge. Scott, keep on the main arrest story. I would think there would be some credentials to confirm on McKay."

At that moment, Tierney's cell phone buzzed. She spoke for a minute, then ended the call.

"That was Mrs. Patton," Tierney announced. "She's coming over here. Says she has some information from the sheriff on her missing broach."

Will moved into action. He knew he needed to notify the pressroom of a late page edit. He checked to ensure the photographer was nearby because he would need art for the article, and he had to rework the front page, leaving space for the new centerpiece story. Although he wasn't certain, Will instinctively knew Barbara Patton was bringing his new lead story.

"Emily," Will instructed. "Go standby at the police station. We will need a statement."

Emily grabbed her notebook and recorder, stood, and headed for the door. She bumped into Barbara Patton, who was coming in. Emily stepped back, apologized, and raced out the door. Seeing Will Hutton, Barbara made a straight line for him. He gestured her to sit down in a chair at an empty desk. She handed him a few official-looking papers. He read them a few times, said something to Mrs. Patton, then motioned for Tierney to come into his office. He handed her the papers. She and Will sat down, facing Mrs. Patton in the glass-enclosed office. With a warm smile, Mrs. Patton spoke first.

"I thought it would be more ethical if I brought this to the Daily Star first," Mrs. Patton said.

"Mrs. Patton," Will said. "The fact you brought this report to us first says a lot. We really appreciate this." He slid an extra chair beside Mrs. Patton, then walked back to his desk and sat.

Tierney walked in slowly, bearing a quizzical look and her reporter's notebook. Will pointed to a chair. Tierney smiled nervously and sat down next to Mrs. Patton, who offered her a warm greeting. Mrs. Patton's rich voice calmed Tierney.

"Let me bring you up to date on the questions you asked last time. First, the broach's value has been set at $10,000 by the insurance company. I would have thought more, but sincc we had no receipt, we were forced to defer to their estimate," Mrs. Patton said with a resigned nod. "Secondly, we will drop the insurance claim once the broach is returned to us undamaged. Third, you will want my reaction to this whole incident. I've thought about that quite a lot," she said as she pulled a handkerchief from her bag.

Mrs. Patton took a deep breath and continued.

"Losing my dear, dear mother was the worst nightmare possible. She was literally fine one day, and then within a week, she had passed," she said.

Tierney interrupted the older woman, who gave her a discerning look. "Mrs. Patton, you can take your time."

Will realized that Mrs. Patton had not appreciated Tierney's comment, which she had meant to be consoling. Too bad, he thought, that Tierney would never realize how much her attempt at being conciliatory had insulted the older woman. So, he tried to speak to Tierney.

"Tierney, why don't we let Mrs. Patton finish, then ask our questions."

Tierney bit her lower lip, a sign, he had learned, that his comment had irritated her. Still, outwardly, Tierney simply nodded. Mrs. Patton's eyes told Will she was relieved by his intervention, and she continued.

"Now, knowing that we will have to live that week repeatedly each time we see the broach, and certainly through all the court proceedings, well, it will be a true challenge," Mrs. Patton said softly. "And for what? We would have helped the young man with expenses if he were in such dire straits as to steal. We are, by no means, rich, but we would have worked out something. $10,000 is not enough to lose a career over. He had worked so hard, and Doc Briggs believed in him. Very perplexing," she breathed deeply and closed her eyes.

After a moment of silence, Will asked a question that he rarely asked of the subject of a story. "Mrs. Patton, how would you like us to write this?"

Mrs. Patton thought for a moment. As the publisher's wife of the largest regional newspaper, she, too, realized the gift that Will Hutton had just given her. Further, by the way he asked the question, she realized he would not be relying on that overly anxious Tierney Baynes to write the story alone. His hand would be in it throughout.

She sat still for a moment, then spoke carefully. Barbara Patton knew that her words, like the court case, would live on forever. She also knew she didn't want to be the one making allegations. Her role, she thought, was to simply be grateful.

"Will, you are so generous. Here's what I'd like to say, for the record, 'We thank the police for their thorough investigation. We'd especially like to thank Sheriff Dove Black and Officer Eliot West for their fine work.' That's it. How does that sound?"

Will knew what she was doing, and Tierney's perplexed look told him that once again, "girl-reporter-extraordinaire-in-her-own-mind" missed the deeper context. Will wondered whether Tierney would ever mature as a journalist.

That was one major reason he kept her on obits and had her shadow Emily Scott. Despite Emily's quirky exterior, her heart beat press ink.

Will smiled softly at Mrs. Patton and said, "That sounds just perfect."

Mrs. Patton stood, and so did Will. His raised eyebrows and nod silently told Tierney that she should rise as well. He walked around his desk, to the front with Tierney, and took Mrs. Patton's outstretched hand.

"We will be very sensitive," he said.

"Good." Mrs. Patton said as she released Will's hand and stepped past Tierney into the mail newsroom. Will and Tierney followed.

"I'd like to find Eliot to personally thank him. He was not in the sheriff's office this morning," Mrs. Patton added.

"Uh, I may know where he is," Tierney interjected. "When Emily was in the sheriff's office, she said Eliot took a call and rushed out. Emily said she thought he was headed to the hospital."

"Oh, dear. His dad–Ira–again," Barbara Patton said, furrowing her brow. "That poor family has been through a rough spot–just like us."

Mrs. Patton gave Will a pat on the arm, nodded to Tierney, and left. Tierney stood in the newsroom, transfixed. Will started to duck back into his office, but he didn't make it in time. Tierney spoke, tugging at his shirt sleeve.

"Mrs. Patton said, 'Just like us.' Will, something is odd about this whole thing," she said.

Tierney did not have her typical wild look. Instead, she was focused and calm. Still, Will felt the need to stop her.

"Oh, no you don't," Will said as he jerked free of her grasp.

"But Will, listen for one minute. The dots are connecting," Tierney insisted. "First, Mrs. Patton's mother. Now, Eliot's dad. Both suddenly get sick. It fits what Dr. McKay was saying—patients dying, and they all have one common symptom—hallucinations. And look at the police report. Read it, and think about it," Tierney said.

She shoved past Will to reach his desk first. She picked up the police report. In reading it again, Tierney found the passage again, describing where the broach was found. She pointed that out and handed the report to Will.

He took the report from her, read it several times, flipping from page one to page two and then back again.

"Damn!" Will exclaimed. "This is NOT an arrest report. It's just an incident report. Officially, McKay has not been charged with anything. His name is not mentioned on this report," Will growled, grabbing his cell phone. He pressed a few digits and waited.

Emily Scott answered. She had been waiting in the police station for Sheriff Black's promised four p.m. announcement, and it was almost that time. Still, Emily's trained eye didn't see the flurry of activity that typically accompanied a media event. The few officers and staff in the open squad room seemed to be working routinely, and Sheriff Black was nowhere in sight. Emily's instincts told her something was amiss. That's when Will's phone call jarred her observation. Emily explained to Will what she was not seeing and offered her hunch that something was wrong. Will's next words confirmed her instinctive assessment.

"Emily, I'm looking at this police report." Will's voice was calm, but she sensed the urgency. "It's an incident report, not an arrest report. In fact, there's no mention of arresting or charging anyone. It says the broach has been found."

Emily calculated quickly. She realized that that explained why nothing was happening in the squad room. Sheriff Black had no arrest to announce. Scanning the room, Emily realized the town's only detective was not here either.

"Will," Emily's typically girl-like voice was now three octaves lower and very calm. "The sheriff and his detective are not here. I'll check the jail log, but my hunch is that Ash McKay is not incarcerated. I'll call you shortly."

Will snapped a photo of the police report and texted it to Emily. Then, he turned his attention to Tierney. He was concerned that she would get too excited and miss the whole story, and for once, Will needed Tierney to focus. He wasn't sure what had happened to her in the intervening years between her internship at the Daily Star during her college days and now, but Tierney had lost her willingness to be patient, to analyze. Now, she was full of preconceived notions, and she spent all of her waking hours pursuing those and complaining that he would not let her be a journalist. Will knew he had good reason.

He kept thinking that someday, if he could find that intern journalist who looked at things objectively, who was willing to invest the time and energy in what seemed like droll research, then he would have one hell of a good reporter for the Daily Star. But at this moment, all Will needed Tierney to do was focus on one thing—following up at the hospital. Will raised the police report and pointed to the incident narrative section as he stood beside Tierney.

"Tierney, look at this and listen carefully," Will said deliberately. "The broach was not under Dr. McKay's phone. It was on top of the desk—right in plain sight. If he planned to fence that broach, he would have kept it hidden," Will said. "I need you to go to the hospital and talk to this nurse, the one who found the broach. If he's not there, go to his house. We don't have his name in the report, but someone there will know. Do not show him the report, but tell him you want his story. Got it?"

Tierney nodded and raced to her desk, fumbling through a few papers and reporter's notebooks. Picking up one, she triumphantly marched back to Will, who still stood outside his office door. He realized, in that moment, he was not going to get Tierney focused until he discredited her latest conspiracy theory. He began by mocking her.

"Here it comes, the 'these people shouldn't be dead because I see a conspiracy list,'" Will's sarcasm seemed to be lost on Tierney.

Instead, she flipped through the pages, landing on one in the middle. She pointed to a list of names, numbers, and dates, displayed in neat columns. She pointed to a few names, unaware that Will was looking at the ceiling instead of her notebook.

"29 names. Will, when was RAM? Wasn't it July? Look at this," she tugged at his tie. Will begrudgingly looked down and followed Tierney's finger as she pointed to names, and then across at the dates. "It's a pattern. Five people who make those complaints of hallucinations, seeing things, and weird behavior have died each month since RAM. There have been four this month, so there's one more," She looked up to see Will finally, really thinking about what she was saying.

"Okay, let's say for a split second that I believe there's something to your conspiracy," Will offered. "What about before RAM?" Will asked skeptically.

Tierney was ready for that question. She told Will that she had secretly been counting obits for the last year, but couldn't prove there was a connection between patients who suffered the weird symptoms and their deaths. "I'd have to interview all the families of everyone who died to learn that, and you won't let me."

Will drew a breath to his full height, folded his arms, and shook his head. "And you better not go out and disrupt families. There's no way to prove anything because no one gets an autopsy unless the law requires it."

Although he would not admit it aloud, Will realized, in that moment, that Tierney could have the seed for a valid story, but it would be one he would never invest resources into developing. To prove Tierney's point, they would need a patient who died of these weird symptoms, had no other contributing health complications, and had undergone a post-mortem. It was a tantalizing idea, but totally unrealistic to prove. Right now, Will had to get Tierney back on the current story, which did have "legs" and needed to be done today.

He had to find a way to tell Tierney, give her some angle that would get her mind off dead people and conspiracies. Bellowing at her in the past had served only to have her dig in harder, press more, and waste too much time. So, he stood silently for a moment. That got Tierney's attention.

What Will never realized was that Tierney had a crush on her boss. Although he was twenty years her senior and had been married to the love of his life, he was not a widower with children to raise. However, Tierney Baynes went home each day thinking about Will's crystal blue eyes, surrounded by his dark, black hair. She had memories of him working when she knew he wasn't looking. Tierney knew it was wrong to have any sort of infatuation for her boss. She knew she would never act on her feelings. Further, she felt that someday, she would meet a man of her own. So, when he spoke kindly and smiled her way, Tierney could not refuse him.

"Tierney," Will said softly, "I know you've done a lot of work on this, and you would agree that it would take much more time to flesh this idea into any sort of potential story." He nodded at her. She stared at him. He continued. "Now, what I need you to do is work on the story at hand–the ruby broach. Can you please do that for me?"

Tierney forced herself not to reach up and stroke his face. She really just wanted to melt into his arms and have Will Hutton hold her. But Tierney knew better. "Sure, Will, I'll get on it. To the hospital. Find the nurse," she said sweetly.

Will watched as Tierney stepped back to her desk, gathering her purse, her recorder, and another notebook. She headed for the door, and then at Will's dread, she stopped and turned to face him. He didn't know what was coming next, but it could not be good.

"But, Will. Don't you see? McKay stealing a broach that wouldn't cover even a percent of his college debt makes no sense," Tierney insisted. "His debt only gets paid in full if he stays in rural community medicine for five years."

That shocked Will. Tierney was actually thinking something relevant and good. To his surprise, Will heard himself agreeing with her and asking the next question. "How much have you done on McKay's background? Anything there?"

Flustered and surprised that Will didn't yell at her as he usually did, Tierney stammered.

"Uh, ah, all the school would give me is essentially name, rank, and serial number. These days, they're so afraid of lawsuits everywhere, they won't tell you if anything bad happened."

Will asked about McKay's family.

"Good working class family from upstate New York. I think his mother and step-father must be on their way here now. I tried to call. There was no answer at their house. Mr. McKay's work said he had left for the day," Tierney said.

"Good work. Now, take off and track down that nurse," Will said, and he genuinely felt he had made a breakthrough in his approach to Tierney. He was encouraged that she had done the research on McKay. Maybe there was hope for her yet.

The Lone Mountain Medical Center stood on a hill, its low-slung, one story rock and glass structure cut back into the hillside as if the building itself were part of the rock in the mountains. Someone said that an architect inspired by the work of Frank Lloyd Wright designed Lone Mountain, but that was never confirmed. Nevertheless, the building itself seemed eternal, as if it had always been there and always would be. The people in the community felt that way. For them, this was their lifeline. When the medical facilities provided by the mining companies disappeared many decades ago, Lone Mountain remained. It was one of the few facilities in the country not owned by a "chain."

People who couldn't pay were treated alongside the few who still had some form of private insurance. Medicare and Medicaid patients relied upon Lone Mountain, and despite the growing cuts to both programs and ever-changing regulations, Lone Mountain held fast. Most emergencies were lovingly handled here by medical staff who were the neighbors and families of the patients they treated.

Nodding to the "pink lady" volunteer at the reception desk, Tierney Baynes breezed into the hospital, choosing to take the right turn down the newer wing. The building itself was shaped like a three-sided cross, with the oldest wing that went straight back closed for renovations. The left wing contained critical care and most of the surgical areas, along with a small maternity ward. If Tierney was going to find the nurse, she would look on the general care wing first. Stopping in front a bank of signs on the wall, Tierney tried to determine which way to go to find the nurse and Dr. Ash McKay's desk. She was certain he would not have an actual office, but a space cut out of a treatment room or something. Taking a step backward to study the hallway, Tierney crashed into another person. To her chagrin, it was Eliot West.

"Eliot! What are you doing here?" Tierney exclaimed. "Oh, that's right. Emily said your dad is here. How is he?"

Eliot pushed Tierney away. "Look, I don't have time to chat."

"Is your dad okay?" Tierney said emphatically.

Eliot tried to walk away. "He will be if I can get him to leave. I need to go now."

"Is Doc Briggs treating your dad?" Tierney asked.

Eliot was obviously irritated by Tierney's continued questioning. "You are not writing a story on my family–Leave me alone."

"I am not interested in writing about your family," Tierney said flatly. "I want to talk to the nurse who found Mrs. Patton's broach, and then I want to talk to Dr. Briggs about Dr. McKay.

"Then go find him," Eliot growled.

Eliot tried to push past Tierney, but she stepped into his path.

"Look," Tierney said. "We were wrong about Doc Briggs being someone else. Maybe it was Doctor McKay–giving everyone the wrong medicine bu..." Eliot cut her off. "No, it wasn't–now move."

Tierney stood defiantly. "I'm not moving until you explain that last remark."

"Move!" Eliot demanded.

Eliot maneuvered around Tierney and rushed into his dad's room, where his mother sat at the foot of the bed and his father lay under the sheets. They were supposed to be ready to leave, but instead, his father had given up. In that moment, Eliot realized he had lost the battle to get his father out of Briggs' clutches. His father, who was still considered in his right mind, would not cross his mother. The only hope now would be that Ira West would have enough strength to survive Dr. Briggs' so-called care. One thing Eliot could do was to stay close, to watch Briggs' every move, and to find ways to counter the treatment, the medication he gave Ira.

Eliot fell into the recliner and closed his eyes. Had he been a praying man, Eliot would have asked the Powers That Be to intervene. He didn't speak.

Tierney had watched Eliot go and wondered what he meant. But she told herself that she would look. She had to find that nurse. Looking at her watch, Tierney thought that the shift change had probably happened. Recalling the incident report, Tierney remembered that the broach had been found the afternoon before. So, she thought she might find the nurse on duty. Her plan was to head to the nurses' station and ask. She turned to head there and saw Dr. Oxenbriggs walking in the same direction as Eliot had. Briggs looked harried and a bit nervous. She stepped toward him.

"Hi. Dr. Oxenbriggs?" Tierney asked. "I'm Tierney Baynes of the Daily Star. I'd like to talk to you a moment about your chief resident, Dr. Ash McKay, and that ruby broach."

Briggs was irritated and distracted. "Ms. Baynes, is it? You know I cannot discuss that with you." He tried to walk away, but she followed. Briggs thought of a gnat.

"Dr. Oxenbriggs. I am asking you about your decision–to choose Dr. McKay. What did you see in him that made you choose him as your chief resident?"

Briggs wheeled around and looked down at Tierney. He jutted his hands on his hips. "If I answer your question, will you please let me get back to work? I have patients who are waiting right now."

A bit intimidated by his overbearing response, Tierney looked at him and nodded. Briggs shook his head affirmatively.

"You want to know about McKay? Alright. He has always been dedicated, caring, and very skilled. But I suppose even I cannot see everything about a person. Now, if you will excuse me, I have a patient who needs me." Briggs started to step away from her, but was halted by Tierney's next question.

"Dr. Oxenbriggs. I just have one more question. Did you ever treat Mrs. Langford? Weren't you the doctor of record?" Tierney asked.

Dr. Oxenbriggs sighed and offered her a charming smile. "You said one question. I'm sure that's more than one. Yes, Mrs. Langford was my patient. I hated to lose her because I love my patients. Sadly, I didn't get to be with her when she passed. Now, is that all?"

Briggs pressed forward, and Tierney followed him.

"That would have been hard, I'm sure," Tierney stammered. "Being there when she died, I mean."

Briggs wheeled around to face her, his face intense. "Ms. Baynes, how do you know? Think of it this way, death brings peace and relief from pain and suffering. It is life's greatest gift. Now, I have a patient waiting."

Briggs didn't think Tierney had heard a word he said. Instead, to his ire, she had pulled out her cell phone and snapped off several photos of him. In an icy tone, Oxenbriggs said flatly that she could not use any of those photos for any reason, any time. "DO. YOU. UNDERSTAND?" Briggs said, the words coming out one at a time. When she nodded furiously, he pressed past her and headed off.

Tierney remembered that she had to find the nurse. So, she shook off Briggs' intimidation and calmly walked to the nurses' station. The clerk at the desk smiled broadly until Tierney introduced herself. Then, he became almost unresponsive. He said he was not allowed to give her any information. Tierney persisted in her most charming manner.

"Look, I just want to get the story right," she implored.

"Can you tell me where the broach was found? There's a lot of confusion, and I understand the family had offered a reward to the finder." That last part was not exactly accurate, but Tierney had heard Mrs. Patton say they thought about offering a reward for the return of the broach. She wasn't sure if that had ever been announced publicly. Either way, the clerk at the nurses' station didn't budge. Tierney knew it was time to move on to someone else and a new tactic. She thanked the clerk and left.

She decided to go to the cafeteria, where some nurses may be more relaxed. Since this hospital had no public relations department to handle media requests, Tierney felt anywhere she went was fair game.

CHAPTER 13

Image Through a Mirror Dimly

Ira West had wakened. Etta pushed a button on the side of the hospital bed that elevated his head. Ira did not speak, but his eyes stared toward the ceiling. Eliot had never seen his father look so hopeless. He had tried once more to convince his mother that they had to leave for Ira West to have any chance at life at all. He also realized that Ira had succumbed to Etta's demands about taking that pill.

"Son, you're acting crazy," Etta said. "You cannot tell a doctor what to do."

"Mamma. While I was gone, you gave daddy that pill, didn't you?" Eliot asked.

She didn't exactly answer his question. "I will do what Doc Briggs says to do. He is the medical expert here."

"We have to get him out of here. Now," Eliot demanded.

Shaking his head in disgust, Eliot leaned over the bed, trying to get his father to sit up on his own. Eliot could see that the pill had affected his usually bright eyes and happy face. Etta pulled Eliot away.

"Eliot, leave your daddy be. Can't you see he's unable to

go anywhere? You'll kill him," she demanded.

Eliot turned on her, struggling to control his rage. "And staying here is sure death!"

The door to the room swung open, and Dr. Oxenbriggs strode in, a wide smile on his face.

"My goodness, what do we have here? I don't allow fussing in my hospital," he gently chided.

Etta West practically fell into his arms. "Doc Briggs, I'm glad you're here. Now, everything will be all right."

He guided her to the recliner and helped her sit. He offered her a warm, comforting smile and nodded as if to say everything would be all right. Then, Briggs took a few steps forward to the bed. He pulled out his stethoscope and deftly began to move it across Ira's chest. He slid the stethoscope into the outside pocket of his lab coat, then reached into the breast pocket and pulled out a small, bright penlight, turned on the light, and shined it into Ira's eyes.

"Your heart is racing a bit, Ira," Dr. Briggs said softly. "Want me to see what I can do about it?"

Ira didn't respond, but Eliot spoke.

"Can we get a cardiologist in here?" Eliot said.

Unfazed, Dr. Briggs continued, "Of course, if you want another doctor, I'll help you arrange one, Ira. After all, you're my favorite patient, and I only want what's best."

In a whisper, Ira said a few words that didn't make sense, and his words trailed off. "You...."

Elliot pleaded with his father. "Daddy, please."

Dr. Briggs patted Ira on the arm. "Well, I'm glad that's settled once and for all. Now, let's get some fluids into you, Ira. Etta, why don't you take Eliot and get a cup of coffee. When you get back, Ira will be much better."

Dr. Briggs turned to Eliot and spoke in a whisper. "Your mother needs a break from the stress of this. Take her for a walk or cup of coffee."

Eliot realized he had lost control entirely. There was nothing he could do or say at this point. At least if he took his mother out of the room, he would ensure that she could not give Ira any more of those pills. So, he turned to his mother, whose worried, yet triumphant look said everything. If Ira took a turn for the worse or died, Eliot would know his conscience was clear. He had fought the good fight and lost to his mother's emotions and his father's love for her. As much as he hated to give up, Eliot realized this was his father's life and his decision. Eliot stood by the recliner as his mother slowly rose.

Bypassing Eliot, she walked to the bed and kissed Ira softly on the head. She offered Dr. Briggs a forced smile, then turned and walked out the door. Eliot followed her. As he reached the exit, he turned to glare at Dr. Briggs, who still stood placidly looking at Ira. Eliot felt so helpless. He wanted to stay, to shove that look right down Dr. Briggs' throat, grab his father, and run as fast and far as possible. But he had lost, and even worse, Eliot could not help the one man he loved more than anyone in the world.

Dr. Oxenbriggs stood in the quiet room, listening to Ira West struggle to breathe. Every few seconds, Ira raised a shaking arm, pointed to the empty space above his head, and blurted out some jumbled words. It appeared as if he were trying to fight off some invisible foe.

Briggs knew he had plenty of time, so he watched Ira struggle. That was always the part he looked forward to with his patients, for their struggle confirmed for Briggs that this patient would be better off dead. Then, Oxenbriggs pulled the IV pole closer to the bed. A bag of clear saline solution hung on the pole. The contents of that bag were harmless. Ira West now lay motionless, his eyes closed. Dr. Oxenbriggs ripped open the syringe end of the IV line and carefully plunged the needle into a vein on the top of Ira's hand. The man barely winced. Dr. Oxenbriggs then slid open the external valves, and the clear saline solution began to drip into the clear plastic lines and slowly slide into Ira's vein. Dr. Briggs noticed that the IV line was extra-long.

To ensure that the syringe would remain in Ira's hand, Briggs taped the syringe securely on Ira's hand and then tucked the excess plastic tubing beneath the sheet that covered Ira's lifeless arm. Dr. Briggs watched the saline solution drip into the tubing and then flow into Ira's hand. After another moment, the doctor pulled a small, fluid-filled syringe from his lab coat pocket. Holding it up to the light, Briggs squirted a drop or two out into the air and flicked the plastic container to ensure there were no air bubbles. Those could be deadly. After all, he wanted to take away his patient's agony.

"Ira, this will all be over, and you will be at peace," Briggs said as he patted Ira's shoulder.

At that moment, Ira flung his free hand into the air, knocking the syringe from Briggs' hand and sending it flying onto the floor. Startled, Briggs stumbled backward and immediately began chasing the syringe as is rolled and tumbled along the concrete floor. He fell to the floor on his knees and finally caught the syringe. Briggs quickly recovered his balance, stood up, brushed off his jacket, and held the syringe up to examine it.

"Good," he said breathlessly, "there's still enough."

Looking down at Ira, Briggs breathed a sigh of relief. That last outburst was nothing more than the Haldol reacting inside his body. That was over, and in a moment, Ira would know eternal peace. Briggs found a port on the side of the plastic IV tubing and plunged the contents of the syringe into it. He watched Ira, as a cat watches a trapped rat. Some of his patients had convulsed when the drug entered their bodies. Some gasped. Then, there was Ira West, who rose up and gulped one last mouth of air. Then, he fell back onto the pillow, still and silent.

Dr. Briggs patted Ira's shoulder and looked for a memento, something to help him love his patient forever. But he found nothing. So, he pocketed the syringe and told Ira goodbye. Then, he whispered, "Death is such a gift."

Cracking open the door to the hallway, Briggs glanced outside to ensure the hallway was empty. Then, just like he had done many, many times, Briggs slipped out undetected. His packed bags waited out in his pick-up truck. He planned to go by his house to gather the remainder of his clothes. Then, he would spend the weekend somewhere far away, deciding where to go next.

On Monday, Briggs would return to the hospital and resign. He would have a convincing story about having achieved all of his goals. He would add that he was proud of all the people who had come after him and say how good he felt about the work they had done together. He would wipe away a tear, hug a few people, and drive off into the shadows of the mountains. This plan had worked in three other cities—all much larger than here in Southwest Virginia. His biggest decision would come this weekend. Where should he go next? Who needed his special love and abilities to know who should live and who should die?

By the time Dr. Ash McKay and Sheriff Dove Black rushed into Ira West's room, long shadows spilled across the floor and over the bed, where Ira West lay motionless. Ash McKay pushed past the sheriff, scrambling to find a stethoscope and equipment to examine Ira.

"Damn. Damn!" Ash exclaimed. "Why didn't you let me come sooner?"

"No time for that now," Sheriff Black stood, watching. "Is he dead?"

Ash waived him off, trying to listen to Ira's heart and breathing.

"Stand by," Ash said curtly. Frantically, he followed the line of the IV and then uncovered Ira's arm, which he carefully lifted to pull the end of the plastic tubing loose. He led it in the air.

Sheriff Black stretched to see what the doctor was doing, and Ash pushed him back.

Ash chuckled. "Well, you sly devil!"

"What the hell is going on?" Sheriff Black demanded. He watched in astonishment as Dr. McKay placed his hand behind Ira's back and helped him sit up in the bed. It was then that Ira pulled his right hand from beneath the covers. He was holding a severed IV line. Ira, too, began to laugh. Ash took the two halves of the tubing in his hand, still chuckling as he spoke.

"How in the hell were you able to cut the line, Mr. West?" Ash asked.

"Well, I pretended to have one of those fits—which I've had too many of now. That knocked the syringe out of Doc Briggs' hand. While he was trying to retrieve it, I sliced the line with my trusty pocket knife. I stuck one end into the bed, and then I laid right still. I didn't take that last pill either," Ira said triumphantly.

Sheriff Black pushed his hat back on his head and scratched his forehead. He began to laugh. "Well, I'll be. I've seen some pretty slick cons in my life, but Ira West, you beat them all," Sheriff Black shook his head.

Ash stood perfectly still for a minute. "Jesus! What about Doc Briggs? He doesn't know we're on to him, does he?" Ash McKay turned to Ira. "Ira, let's get you up now."

"Ah, I'm fine now," Ira announced, swinging his feet over the side of the bed to the floor and tossing off the hospital gown. To everyone's surprise, Ira was fully dressed, right down to his shoes. He tried to stand on wobbly legs, and Sheriff Black and Dr. McKay grabbed his arms and sat him back down on the bed.

"You sit right here, and I'll get a nurse," said Dr. McKay.

Ira shook his head. "Doc, if you don't mind, I'd like to find my wife and my son. They are somewhere here in the hospital. I've had quite enough of this place. Mind if I call them?"

Sheriff Black handed Ira the desktop phone that was on the night stand nearest him. "That's a good idea," he said. "Meanwhile, you need to show me something, Dr. McKay."

The sheriff gestured for McKay to move the IV pole closer to the fading light of the window. When Ash had done that, the Sheriff turned his back to Ira on the bed. "I wanted to ask you if the drug would still be in evidence in this bag or Ira's body, Dr. McKay," the sheriff whispered.

"Not likely, sir," Ash replied. "I would recommend that you keep this for evidence, and save the bed sheets as well."

"Well, I'll call in the state on this one, but the chain of custody has been destroyed, so I don't suppose we will be able to prove much," Sheriff Black bemoaned.

"Sheriff," Ash questioned. "I don't understand this at all. I thought all you had to do is know the doctor had done this and you could go arrest him."

Sheriff Black shook his head. "That's what everyone thinks, but you have to prove a person committed the crime, and the evidence has to connect the crime to that person."

"Very complicated," Ash said.

At that moment, a very shocked Etta West, closely followed by Eliot, shoved the door open and ran to Ira's bed.

"What is going on? Where is Doc Briggs? Why is HE here?" Etta demanded in a flood of questions.

"Hey, Etta," Ira chimed in a lyrical voice, "I'm alive. I'm fine. Thanks for asking. Oh, and Dr. McKay saved my life."

A chorus of astonished "what's?" and "how's?" filled the room until Ash broke in.

"Well, I didn't exactly save you, Mr. West," Ira said. "Seems you saved yourself. I do need to know, Ira. What prompted you to take action?"

"It was something about the way Doc Briggs wanted me to take that pill all the time and told me I was his favorite patient," Ira explained. "Nobody loves me that much. Just ask my wife," Ira joked, nudging Etta in the side.

Sitting on the bed beside her husband, Etta jumped when Ira poked her. "What did you do, Ira?"

"Mrs. West, you don't need to worry now," Ash said. "Your husband is strong and will recover now. In fact, Mr. West prevented a deadly drug from getting into his system."

"Which drug? I want to know exactly what happened here!" Etta demanded.

"It's the same medication as those pills Doc Briggs had you give your husband. He will recover now if you don't give him any more of those pills," Ash warned.

Etta stood. "I still don't understand. I ask you again, where is Doc Briggs?"

Sheriff Black, who had been uncharacteristically quiet, stepped forward. "Eliot, you should stay with your folks. Me and the other guys can handle this."

Ira tried to stand again, this time with a bit more strength. "Ah, no. I've had enough hovering to last a lifetime. If it's all the same to you, Doc McKay and Sheriff, I want to go home. Eliot can get back to work."

They all looked at Dr. McKay. He studied Ira for a moment, then nodded. "Okay, but if you have any symptoms—go straight to Kingsport. And Mrs. West, give me those pills, and throw away the ones you have at home."

Etta still looked shocked. "Ira, you are Doc Briggs' patient."

Ira took her hand and focused on his wife's face. She was afraid. He had to calm her, to help her understand. His voice was soft.

"Etta, honey. Will you just take me home, please? I am going to be fine. I need you to do what the doctor here says. He is the one who saved me. The rest doesn't matter at the moment."

Ira stared at her, watching her think through what he had said and finally agree. She nodded, took his hand, and started out the door. Eliot stopped them.

"I think you'll need these," he said, tossing the keys to Ira, who caught them in one swift move. "Mamma, you will not call Doc Briggs."

After a moment, she looked at her son and her husband and nodded reluctantly.

"Oh, Doc McKay, do I need to make an appointment or something to see you?" Ira asked.

Ash shook his head. "I still have a few things to clear up with the sheriff—and I need to make sure I can get my program finished."

"You mean you cannot see me?" Ira asked.

"As far as me, you're clear," Sheriff Black said. "The

medical part, I have no control over whatsoever."

Ira smiled. "You will make it, Doc, and I'll be your loyal patient," he said, turning toward the door. "Etta, let's go home."

Eliot watched his parents disappear into the hallway, and then he turned to Sheriff Black. "We should be looking for Doc Briggs."

Sheriff Black paced the room for a moment, rubbing his chin and nodding. He turned to Doc McKay, "Wouldn't he be expecting to be called to Ira West's room?"

Ash walked to face Sheriff Black. He told the sheriff that the call typically came much sooner and that coming so much later might make Briggs suspicious. Ash could tell that the sheriff wanted the call made, so he relented. He walked to the bed and pushed the nurse call button.

"Hi, this is Dr. McKay. Could you please page Dr. Briggs to room 119?" McKay said. "They will page him," McKay told the sheriff. "Do you think he will be suspicious? What will I say?"

"Whatever you can to get him off kilter a bit. Say they've taken Ira West already and you just had some questions about what to write on the death certificate—or that the family wants an autopsy," Sheriff Black responded. "We will be just inside the bathroom."

"I really want to clobber him," Ash said, looking at his watch. "It's been a while. Do you think he's suspicious?"

"It's possible," Sheriff Black nodded. "I don't think he's ever come this close to being found out."

"Ever come this close?" Eliot asked. This last statement caught him by surprise. After all, Sheriff Black had defended the incredible Dr. Briggs so vehemently, even threatening to fire Eliot if he tried to look into Briggs at all.

Sheriff Black nodded. "Doc Briggs is too practiced, too smooth. He's done this before," the Sheriff said flatly.

The anger burst out, and Eliot heard himself cursing Sheriff Black. "How in the hell could you do this? You are lower than low, you asshole! To let me think you trusted that damn doctor and prevented me from doing what I could to stop him. Damn you!"

When he realized what he had done, Eliot immediately reached for his badge and gun and carefully handed the gun, handle first, to Sheriff Black, and then he jutted the badge toward the hulk of a man. To Eliot's surprise, Sheriff Black stood silently, staring down at him with his hands by his side. After a moment of that cold stare, Eliot withered.

"Sheriff," Eliot said quietly, "I was out of line. I am sorry. I will resign if you wish."

Still, the sheriff stood silently, still staring at Eliot. The look was broken by a nurse entering the room. She looked shocked and surprised. Ash McKay was the first to break the silence.

He asked her calmly, "Did you find Dr. Oxenbriggs?"

"Un, ah, no, Dr. McKay," she stumbled over her words. "He, ah, didn't answer the page."

Ash gestured softly and carefully toward the door as the curious nurse gazed around the room, trying to make sense of the empty bed, the doctor, and the two police officers standing there. She had heard about the broach, of course, and that Ash had been arrested. So, she wondered, why was he standing here in an empty room with the sheriff and a deputy? "There must be some story behind all this," she thought. But she would not learn more. Ash moved to the room's door and ushered her out.

She made her way back toward the nurses' station on the other end of the hallway, where she was met by none other than Tierney Baynes. The nurse had never met the reporter before and was even more stunned to have the blubbering girl pepper questions at her.

"Hi, I'm Tierney Baynes with the Daily Star," Tierney said cheerily. "I'm working on the story of the ruby broach that was found here in the hospital, and I was hoping to see where it was found and to have the nurse who found it tell me what happened."

The nurse had been so overwhelmed by what she had just left, she didn't stop to think about the hospital's policy regarding talking to the media. She knew exactly where that broach was found, and she had heard details from the nurse who found it.

"Sure, let me show you Dr. McKay's desk," the nurse said. "It's right down here."

She led the way down a side hallway and through a doorway that led to a private, open room, where several desks were arranged in a quad. Each one had two nameplates, including the farthest one, which had Dr. McKay's name on a brown easel-like sign.

"It was right here," the nurse gestured to the middle of the desk, "setting right in the open on top of everything."

"Really?" Tierney asked. "I heard it was under his cell phone, sort of hidden?"

The nurse shook her head. "No, that's not right. I know that for sure."

"Who found it?" Tierney pressed on.

"It was Rick DeCaro, second shift," the nurse explained. "Dr. McKay asked Rick if he would come get his cell phone for him, and Rick found the broach on top of the phone."

"Is Mr. DeCaro on duty?" Tierney felt she was on a roll and pushed out as many questions as possible.

"Oh, I don't think so," the nurse responded. "We work four on and four off, so I think he's off now."

"I'll bet it was quite a shock for you," Tierney said, "you know, learning that the person who stole the ruby broach that everyone in town talked about works right here in the hospital."

"Well, you are right," the nurse took a deep breath as she

placed a hand on her stomach. "It was very scary. We've never had anything like that happen here that I know of. Lone Mountain is a good place, and we know everybody. I didn't want to come into work today at all, but I have to make a living."

Excited that she had the information she came for, Tierney snapped a couple of photos of Dr. Ash McKay's desk. She asked the nurse for a photo, but she declined. The nurse also turned down Tierney's request for Rick DeCaro's address. Looking at her watch, Tierney realized the window to get this story into tomorrow's edition was quickly closing. She raced toward the entrance of the hospital, jumping into her car as she called Will to give him the good news.

However, Will seemed less than impressed after Tierney told him she had not asked the nurse her name. Tierney considered the mistake for a moment and told herself the nurse's name didn't matter that much to the story. In fact, the only thing that mattered was that Tierney would have the lead story because she had gotten the details about finding the broach.

She punched a few keys on her cellphone and found Rick DeCaro's address over in Pennington Gap. That was good half hour drive across the curvy Highway 58. Tierney would have to hurry. She was grateful for modern technology that would allow her to email the story and the photos straight to the story bin. She knew this story would get her out of the obit graveyard.

Meanwhile, in room 119, the tense standoff between Eliot and Sheriff Black had ended peacefully, with Black blustering past Eliot and telling him that he could not accept his resignation. To Eliot's relief, the sheriff said he would deal with the insubordination later, but for now, they had a case to work. Eliot put his gun back into its holster and pinned his badge back onto the breast pocket of his uniform.

After all the time they had waited, it was clear to Sheriff Black, Eliot, and Ash McKay that Briggs was not coming. He had apparently sensed something was amiss and fled.

Sheriff Black's radio crackled, and pulling it from his waist belt, the Sheriff spoke into the handheld two-way.

"So, he hasn't come home?" the sheriff questioned. "And he's not here at the hospital either."

Sliding the radio back onto his belt, the Sheriff turned to Eliot. "Looks like the best doctor in town has left us."

"Sheriff, sir," Eliot started slowly. "I checked his employment record and talked to his last supervisor. If Briggs had done anything, they never let on at all."

Ash McKay answered first. "That's how it's done these days. No hospital wants to risk a lawsuit over a bad reference." Ash turned to Sheriff Black, "Look, can't we just have him arrested and put out one of those all points bulletins or something? Why can't you just arrest him?"

Ash looked at Eliot in shock. "What about Ira West's experience? The drug? It's in the IV lines? And what about the broach and the box of jewelry Oxenbriggs stashed in the hospital?"

Eliot shrugged. "I tried to tell you, Doc. That's all circumstantial."

Sheriff Black nodded in agreement. "The most we have are suspicions, and those are not sufficient enough to get an arrest, much less win a case in court. Anyway, why don't you show me this so-called private room the doctor kept?"

Eliot suggested the sheriff call the state crime scene unit to collect any evidence in room 119, and Sheriff Black said they were on their way. He didn't hold out much hope of any evidence that would link Briggs to a crime. Out in the main hospital corridor, the odd-looking trio received more than their share of quizzical looks and whispered comments as they passed by. Dr. McKay tried to hide his nervous energy, but he could feel his body quivering. He feared two things—either they would find Briggs or they would not. If they had to face the great doctor, he would know that Ash was to blame. If Briggs was not there, then how could Ash prove his allegations? He would be right back where he started, with a lot of suppositions and no evidence.

They were now in the darkened, dusty hallway. It seemed longer than ever, and the room that Dr. Briggs used stood silent and dark on the far end. As they entered, led by Ash, he realized they would find nothing. He pushed open the secret drawer of the desk. The scrapbook wasn't there. Rushing over to the nightstand, he lifted and shook it to open the hidden panel. Nothing. Frantically, Ash paced the room. His worst nightmare had come true. He dreaded facing Sheriff Black because he would now go back to jail for stealing a broach he had never seen before. And he was sure to lose his position here at the hospital and still owe for all those loans.

"My life is over," Ash heard himself blurting out.

"What?" Eliot asked. "What are we supposed to see here, Dr. McKay?"

"It was here," Ash screamed in agony, rushing back and forth from the desk to the night stand.

Sheriff Black watched Ash for a moment or two, then stepped in front of him. "Son, son," the sheriff said. "Listen, I need you to calm down and help me. Can you do that?" He gave Ash a calming, warm look.

Ash looked frantically about the room, breathed deeply, and closed his eyes. The sheriff patted Ash's arm and gently shook him. He gave Ash a consoling, reassuring look.

"Son, you are not responsible for Doc Briggs," Sheriff Black offered softly. "It's clear that he was up to something, or he would not have left so abruptly. Okay now?"

"But sheriff," Ash said, "both you and Eliot have warned

me too many times that we need proof to arrest the 'best doctor in town', and everything is gone. And that broach was found on my desk."

"Dr. McKay, you were also the one who convinced me that you were worried about your patients," Eliot chimed in.

Sheriff Black moved carefully around the room, examining the hidden compartment in the night stand and the fake bottom in the drawer of the desk.

Finally, he spoke. "The most that you can do here is maybe a malpractice lawsuit against the doctor, and that would be for the West family to decide."

"We have no proof Doc Briggs ever did anything illegal," Eliot added.

"What about the broach?" Ash asked.

"No one saw him with it, and so far, we have no fingerprints, no DNA to link him to the piece," Eliot added.

"And even after the crime lab folks get done with the hospital room, a good lawyer could easily make the point that Oxenbriggs had every right to touch anything in the room and that he saw the broach on Mrs. Langford at some point," Sheriff Black said.

"I lose my career, and the 'best doctor in town' walks off into the sunset. Damn!" Ash complained.

Sheriff Black walked out of the room. Eliot and Ash quickly followed. "Is there another way out of this hallway?"

Sheriff Black asked.

Ash thought for a moment and then remembered the old stairwell that led to the basement and to the outside. He gestured for the police officers to follow him and led them down the dark stairs to the basement. Sheriff Black and Eliot had each pulled out very bright flashlights that lit their way to the damp, silent basement and out the doorway into the fading light of the evening. Black turned back into the basement, flicked on his flashlight, and walked around inside the space. Pipes and vents ran the length of the ceiling. The dusty concrete floor was cracked in many places.

Black saw nothing to indicate that another person had been in the basement at all. He could not show that he was disappointed or angry that he had been out maneuvered by a doctor. He vowed to himself that he would find that guy someday and give him what he deserved. But for now, he had one task: to get his town back in order. The first step would be making a statement for that damnable paper that everyone seemed to read despite the Internet.

CHAPTER 14

The Image Clears

To her great disappointment, the full story that Tierney wrote about the discovery of the broach was never published. Since she never talked to Rick DiCaro and all her information came from a nurse who actually witnessed nothing, that never made it into the story. In fact, only a sentence or two of Tierney's reporting ended up on the front page. The lead story carried Emily's byline first and Tierney's in a footnote that said she had contributed to the story.

The story that Emily wrote focused on the return of the broach by "hospital staff." The sheriff was quoted, saying that Dr. Ash McKay had never been charged with a crime of any sort, but rather, he had helped the police investigate the theft.

As Will read Emily's story, he stopped for a question. "Emily, did Sheriff Black ever say what convinced him that McKay was telling the truth?" Will asked.

Without looking up from her keyboard, Emily answered. "It's right there in my piece. Basically, McKay was so concerned about people dying, the sheriff didn't buy that he was the thief. Also, Black was suspicious of the broach being out in the open like that."

Will pulled the line up in the story and read through it on his computer screen. "Scott, you need to put that in quotes attributed to the sheriff." He hit a key or two on the keyboard, sending the story back to Emily. "You need to rewrite," Will instructed.

As she scanned the electronic rundown and found her story, Emily saluted Will and intently began to write again.

Will kept staring at his computer screen, alternately reading and punching keys. He did not look up but yelled across the room, "Baynes. The obit file. Now!"

Tierney was walking back from the front desk, holding a handful of paper obituaries, when she heard Will yelling. She was so tired of writing the lowest column at the paper, tired of Will's low expectations of her abilities, and tired of not getting any respect. This time, she decided to speak out. "Nothing changes. I bring down a killer doctor—"

Will, still working at his desk, cut her off. "Killer doctor! No! If you mean Doc Briggs, he's gone. Broke a lot of hearts—to leave without a word. Suspicious, yes. Killer—no proof."

Tierney bypassed her desk and with the obits in hand, marched into Will's office. She was mad. "Will, you must admit that it was the dates of those 29 deaths. Several occurred before McKay arrived. That proved to you he wasn't the killer," Tierney stomped her feet and shook the handful of papers at him.

Typing away, Emily chimed in, "She's right, Will."

Mrs. Patton's statement saying that she had been grateful for the fine work of the police department made it into the article. Dr. McKay made a statement as well, saying that his priority had been patient care. The hospital president also spoke, saying the police had done a "monumental job" by finding the broach so quickly and that she was glad her staff had been so helpful.

The day after that story appeared, the biggest story in recent history hit the front page. In it, the hospital announced that Dr. Oxenbriggs had left to take "some well-deserved time away." The hospital president added that all the initiatives that Dr. Oxenbriggs had started would continue, including the community clinics, the medical recruiting, and even his dedication to RAM. She added that the residents would finish their program as well.

Yet, an earthquake could not have devastated the community more. Dr. Briggs' decision to leave abruptly was the talk of the town, undercut by suspicious that something had been wrong for him to "just up and leave like that."

Eliot's mother cried when she read the news. For a couple of days, she refused to speak to Eliot, blaming him for "running off Doc Briggs." Ira said to just let her be and she would come around. He half-jokingly told Eliot that he had known Etta a little longer and to trust him. Eliot finally stopped trying to convince her that the great physician was not the best doctor in town and likely had been the cause of several untimely deaths. Etta refused to hear that. She told Eliot that she would not forgive him if he said any more negative things about Dr. Oxenbriggs.

Eliot decided to let his mother keep her delusion, realizing that Briggs was gone and could not harm his father further. So, he hugged Etta and said in all sincerity that she could believe in the goodness of Dr. "Briggs" Oxenbriggs if that helped her.

For the few days after the Oxenbriggs story, Will and his team created what he knew would be award-winning coverage. They wrote stories on the doctor who had been on staff the whole time and was excited to assume control over community clinics. Saying she was committed to providing the best medical care to the people in Wise, Lee, and surrounding counties, the hospital president assumed control of the community medicine recruiting program, and she said a new doctor would be on staff soon to run the RAM integration program.

Will had let Tierney write a sidebar piece on the future of the recruiting program. With UVA-Wise so close, the Coastal Virginia Medical University agreed to send a fully-accredited teaching professional to oversee the program and teach from the Wise campus. It meant that Ash and the rest of the residents would get to finish their program at Lone Mountain Medical Center.

Ash McKay read the article and knew he would complete the work and try his best to stay in these mountains. He had come to love the people, and the work made a difference every day.

Will's team also wrote a retrospective featuring medical care during the heyday of coal mining. These included features about the world-class hospital at Stonega, doctors who made house calls, and interviews with people who remembered them.

Tierney pushed Will to let her write the story she'd been aching to do for six months. Those 29-dead people who all shared those weird symptoms still needed a story.

"Will, I can interview the families now, please," she begged Will, who didn't even look at her.

"The lab results came in on Ira West's pills. They were Haldol. Ira West and his attorney have agreed to let me interview them this week. The pills were Haldol, prescribed by Oxenbriggs," Tierney said.

Will never looked at Tierney. "Convincing, but since we could never prove that the deaths were anything other than normal, there's no proof they were connected."

Tierney pressed him, saying she should be able to talk to the families now. Since Briggs' leaving had created a kind of mass hysteria, interviews would not be noticed.

"Tierney, how many times do I have to tell you?" Will said flatly, "That's malpractice if they ever find him, and I don't think the cops are working too hard on that score."

Emily had finished the rewrite of her story and stood to stretch. "The hospital certainly doesn't want him found–his reputation is now in question, at the least. It's sad all those people died, but he's right T. We have no proof."

CHAPTER 15

Hard Decisions

Luvena Robbins still could not get used to the idea that Frank was not going to be there when she got home from work. After he passed away at the hospital the month before, Luvena lived in a sort of fog for a while. Nothing seemed real, as if she were walking in a long, eternal nightmare. At the funeral, people hugged her, cried with her, and held her as she sobbed, but she didn't remember any of them. Did her daughter come to the funeral? Luvena had no idea. She did know her daughter had not called since the day Frank was buried. Luvena figured it was because Marion knew there was no money to have, and she certainly didn't want the children. That last thought was a relief to Luvena. She needed those kids with her now, and they were finally secure.

To her surprise, after Frank's death, Luvena had found work as a waitress at the new restaurant that opened downtown. She worked during the morning and lunch trade, which were the busiest, so that she could work when her grandchildren were in school. They were finally getting some financial help from child services, and that made providing for her grandchildren easier. They even had health insurance, and because she would turn 65 in a year, she would be able to get Medicare.

She still hated the silence and emptiness of coming home. She always arrived before the children's bus. Occasionally, she had a feeling that she heard Frank's laughter or his footsteps somewhere as she drank her morning coffee or sat in the silence of her bedroom at night after the children had drifted off to their dreams. Luvena wanted to call out to him, to tell him about her day, ask his advice, and to share with him the delights of the grandchildren. But people would think her crazy for having such thoughts, so Luvena remembered the times with Frank and cried alone in the tiny living room of the white, wood-framed house that she and Frank had bought years ago in a more secure and prosperous time for the Robbins family and the region. Everything about it reminded Luvena of Frank.

The house sat on the top of a green knoll, with a winding driveway that Frank and a neighbor had graded with the neighbor's machinery. Then, they flattened and poured gravel along the even, dirt bed. Luvena crossed over vestiges of those original gravel each day as she drove to and from home. The driveway ended at the front porch, a battleship grey, plank board that stretched the length of the house. A white screen door framed a solid, wooden, blue door.

That door opened into a neat living room, simply decorated with a tan, two-seater couch, a rocking chair, and a puffy recliner. That had been where Frank sat most of the time. They didn't have a television in the living room, preferring to spend their time together talking or reading.

The living room opened to a small dining room, where a dark, mahogany dining room set filled the space. The set had been a wedding gift from Frank's family when he and Luvena married. Of course, it had been his grandmother's dining room set, so handing it down to the new couple signified that Frank's parents approved of the match and believed in their success.

Frank and Luvena had spent most of their time in the kitchen at the red, Formica-topped table and faux leather covered chairs. Luvena still set the table for six sometimes, and then she remembered he was gone and hurriedly took up the place setting before the children bounded into the kitchen.

The official looking letter arrived one month after the day that Frank had been buried. When she pulled the mail out of her box at the bottom of her driveway, Luvena held it for a moment, deciding whether she had the strength to open it. The return address was the Virginia Medical Examiner's office in Richmond. Luvena both dreaded and anticipated the contents of this particular envelope. She forced herself to go home, to keep to her routine, and to wait until the children were well asleep before she opened the envelope.

Shaking and fighting the urge to rip the envelope open at every moment, Luvena kept to her plan, with one exception. When she had changed from her work uniform, she poured herself a cup of coffee, sitting quietly at the kitchen table with the envelope facing her. She tried to think of what she should do, but her mind raced. This envelope contained the results of the autopsy she had agreed to have performed in a moment of great grief and pain. Cutting on a dead person was a desecration, and this letter contained proof of her sin. She feared it would detail exactly the manner in which Frank's body had been poked, prodded, and defiled. Luvena did not want to read any of that. However, she wanted to know exactly what killed her beloved husband.

All those stories in the paper indicated that Dr. Oxenbriggs had run off—left town in a hurry, as Luvena interpreted the stories. She may not have gone to college, but she could read between the lines, and these suggested that Dr. Oxenbriggs had not been entirely honest. Therefore, Luvena really wanted to know if he had a hand in Frank's early death.

After a moment, Luvena knew what she would do. She remembered that young doctor, the one who convinced her to approve of the autopsy in the first place. She would call him, and tomorrow after work, Luvena would take the unopened envelope to the hospital and have him read it to her. She could leave it for that long and then rest easy that he would give her the results and spare her the details.

The next afternoon, Luvena Robbins waited nervously in a small, well-appointed meeting room at the Lone Mountain Medical Center. She gingerly held the envelope in front of her, then placed it onto a small, wooden table that sat between the two upholstered chairs in the room. She sighed and paced, then tried to sit. She examined her work uniform to ensure it had no food spots. She hated that she hadn't taken a proper change of clothes to wear for this meeting.

The door opened, and Dr. Ash McKay stepped inside and closed the door behind him. The moment of reckoning was at hand. Luvena drew a breath. Dr. McKay offered her a kind, warm smile and stretched his hand toward her in greeting. She took his hand, and he held her quivering hand for a moment.

She looked into his face and saw his sincerity and kindness. She turned, picked up the envelope, and handed it to him. She bit her lip while he opened it and began to scan the contents of the four pages.

"What does it say?" Luvena asked anxiously. "And I don't want to know all of what they did to my Frank."

"Okay, let's see. It says he died from a massive dose of the drug, Haldol," Dr. McKay said. "Mrs. Robbins, that's the medicine for schizophrenia, and we know that your husband was not schizophrenic."

She began to cry, and he allowed her to rest her shaking head against his shoulder. The idea that her husband had died at the hands of the doctor they trusted to save him would be a great deal to absorb. So, Dr. McKay let Luvena cry until she was ready to hear more. After a few minutes, her crying waned, and she nodded.

"Is that all?" she asked tearfully.

"No ma'am," Dr. McKay said. "It says that your husband's death was intentional and caused by the overdose."

She cried more and then wiped her eyes and looked at Dr. McKay.

"What happens now?" she asked weakly. "I don't think I can take anything else."

Dr. McKay knew that Luvena Robbins was a strong mountain woman, so when she said she was at her limit, he knew she had suffered all she could. He wanted to comfort her and help her survive this latest shock.

"There's nothing for you to do now," Dr. McKay said softly. "We will turn this information over to the authorities. They will take over from here. Of course, you are encouraged to consult an attorney, as you may have a case against Dr. Oxenbriggs."

Luvena stood silent, staring out the tiny window at the mountains surrounding them, tall silhouettes that enveloped the people here, protecting and isolating them. For

Luvena, she drew her strength from these mountains. When she turned again to face Dr. McKay, Luvena spoke from that mystical power of those mountains.

"Do what needs to be done, Dr. McKay, and I will stand by you," Luvena said. "Frank died unnecessarily, but I am also glad that what killed him will not befall my grandchildren."

"I'm glad you called me, Mrs. Robbins," Dr. McKay said softly. "Whatever is in that envelope, we will face it together."

CHAPTER 16
Answers and Questions

Sometimes, Will liked to be in the newsroom early in the morning to enjoy the relative silence. The only other people there were the receptionist, Mary Ellen, who also functioned as the editor of the community calendar, a sales associate, and Brett, the sales manager. This was one of those days. After greeting Mary Ellen and nodding to Brett, who was leaving for a breakfast meeting, Will wandered through the cool, dark pressroom, with its floor to ceiling machinery, and then into the newsroom. Desks cluttered with papers, books, notebooks, and half-empty water bottles made Will think that an earthquake had interrupted the people who inhabited this space in mid work and they had bolted. On the other hand, Will's office stayed pristine. He craved order. Each day, he spread all his work out, and at the end of the shift, he put each and everything back in place.

As he walked through the newsroom, Will stopped to admire the large, framed papers filling one entire wall. For him, these prize-winning issues reminded Will why this tiny paper in the backwoods of Virginia—a place few people knew existed—meant so much. Even the readers didn't understand the significance of these awards. This paper was their watchdog, their true north, and in the world of journalism, it stood for honesty, credibility, and ethics. This wall kept Will coming back to work and helped to sustain him during the tragic death of his beloved wife. He knew that the work that his tiny, sometimes unruly, team did this last week would one day hang among the winners on this wall.

Will headed to his desk, where he scanned the computer daybook and made some notes on story ideas. His peace was shattered when Emily Scott and her loud, clicking high heels clattered into the newsroom. Aggravated that his peace had been destroyed, Will rose, crossed his office, and deliberately slammed the door. Then, he realized she was talking on the phone, and he wanted to hear what she said. After a moment, Will calmly opened his door and returned to his desk. Fortunately, sound traveled well in the newsroom.

"Oh, yeah, I remember," Emily was saying. "My god. Hey, is this for attribution? Can you e-mail the report to me, please?" Her voice became very excited. "I am in the newsroom and will wait at my desk."

Emily shoved the phone into the pocket of her teal jacket and clacked over to her desk and flopped down, flicking on the computer and drumming her long nails on the metal desktop.

"Ah, ha!" Emily exclaimed in a high-pitched voice.

Will couldn't wait any longer. He marched out into the newsroom and stood over Emily's desk. She was not surprised to see him. In fact, she had known he was in the newsroom all the while. Emily offered him a distracted greeting and rushed over to the printer. She drummed her fingers while she waited, nervously swaying from one foot to the other. When the paper finally slid out of the printer tray, Emily jerked it out and read it furiously.

"AHHHH!" she screamed. "WE GOT HIM!" Emily realized she had been yelling and drew in a deep breath that she exhaled as she ran a finger down the center of her face. "I'm centered. I'm calm."

Will had followed Emily to the printer and anxiously watched through all her gyrations. He grabbed the paper from her hand and read it several times. "Damnation!" he exclaimed. "Now, this is a story."

Emily rushed to her desk to comb through the report, making notes as she scanned the pages one by one. Her work was punctuated every so often with exclamations of "Jesus Howard Christ!" and "How in the world could he!" When Will could no longer stand her outbursts, he stomped over to her desk and grabbed the report.

Towering over Emily, Will read the pages and then,

one-by-one, handed them back to her.

At that moment, Tierney breezed into the newsroom past Will and Emily, who were now earnestly reading the report. Tierney tossed her things onto her desk, then noticed the pair intently reading.

"What do you two have there?" Tierney asked cheerily.

"Huh?" Will asked distractedly.

"I said, what has your attention?" Tierney said more emphatically.

Emily barely looked up but responded to Tierney's question. "There's this man who died at the hospital a few weeks ago. His wife agreed to an autopsy, and the full report just came in."

Tierney grabbed a notebook and flipped through it quickly. "The Robbins–Luvena and Frank, right?"

This time, Emily and Will offered Tierney perplexed looks.

"How did you know?" Emily asked, without waiting for an answer. "Anyway, they finally got the full autopsy report, and it shows that he was given Haldol in massive doses–ordered by Dr. Oxenbriggs. That's what killed him. We have to wait on the coroner's determination that it is murder. Eliot sent this report."

Will swung into action. Tierney loved to see him in this mode because she knew he loved this part of his job the best. Sometimes, Tierney imagined him as a military leader, barking orders and dodging bullets as a battle raged on around him. "Now, we have something to write. Emily, get to the police station. Tierney, to the Robbins family. This is one obit profile that will make the front page," Will ordered.

Tierney and Emily both stopped and considered what had happened. Tierney had been vindicated after all. Those 29 deaths meant something now for sure. All of Tierney's work had not been in vain. Further, this meant one thing, which she announced to the newsroom. "They'll look for Oxenbriggs now. Murder has no statute of limitations."

Emily nodded. She thought about the mountains, those Blue Ridge slopes that she cherished, as contributing factors in the situation that now unfolded. The mountains isolated the people here and created a mythical character for the outside world, the unenlightened mountain man. The people here waited for resources to come to them. Many expected the coal industry to spontaneously rebound any day. They rarely looked beyond these hills to seek resources and often preferred to wait rather than take action.

"If we weren't in such an isolated mountain location, desperate for medical care, could this have happened?" Emily asked.

Will shook his head. "It could happen anywhere. There's the celebrated case in England. Recently, police in Florida arrested a so-called surgeon who had never been to medical school. He had practiced for years in several states."

Triumphantly, Tierney picked up her phone, pushed a few buttons, and opened to a photo of Dr. Briggs. "At least I have a picture of the great Doctor Oxenbriggs. It will go on the wires."

"Why are you still here?" Will demanded. Emily and Tierney grabbed their things and headed out.

At the police station, Eliot West stood reading the Frank Robbins autopsy when Sheriff Black lumbered into the room. He pushed his Stetson back onto his head and stopped to see what held Eliot's attention.

"Ah," Sheriff Black said. "That autopsy report."

"Does this mean we can now go after Oxenbriggs, Sheriff Black?" Eliot asked.

"That's an interesting question," the Sheriff said. "We are waiting on the coroner's report."

"But Sheriff, isn't that just a formality at this point?" Eliot pressed for more information.

The Sheriff explained that once the coroner reviewed the autopsy, it would be most likely that, given the autopsy report, the ruling would be homicide. Then, they could go after Oxenbriggs and conduct a full investigation. What Sheriff Black knew but did not say was that finding Briggs would be challenging—even with all the power of the Internet and social media. Oxenbriggs was a chameleon, practiced in the art of gaining trust. This was the kind of criminal that made people suspend their disbelief and accept his façade of care and concern as the real thing.

By the time that Emily Scott arrived in the police station, the coroner's report had been delivered by e-mail and fax. Sheriff Black, the department detective, and Eliot West read copies.

"Hello," Emily said in her high-pitched, cheery voice. "I am Emily Scott of the Daily Star. I'm here about Frank Robbins' autopsy?"

No one looked up, so Emily stood at the waist-high desk and drummed her long nails on the Formica topped desk. Finally, Eliot could not stand the sound any longer. He leaned toward her and placed his hand on top of Emily's drumming hand. A shot of electricity shot through him, and he realized that came from touching Emily. Even though he had asked her to the prom in high school, until that moment, Eliot West never thought of Emily Scott, the quirky, yet calculating and talented reporter, as a romantic interest. The very thought frightened and intrigued him.

Emily looked up at him and jerked her hand away. "Are you trying to arrest me, officer?" she joked.

"If I were to arrest you, Ms. Scott," Eliot mocked. "You'd know it. So, how can I help you?"

Emily explained that she had come for more information on the Robbins autopsy report and wanted to know whether the coroner's report had arrived. Eliot was impressed with Emily's knowledge of the process and glad that he didn't have to explain everything and then worry that she would write the wrong thing in the paper.

Sheriff Black finally turned to face Emily and Eliot, and she had the feeling the sheriff knew all along that she was there.

"We've only just received the coroner's report, Ms. Scott," Sheriff Black offered. "As soon as I have a chance to review it thoroughly, I'll give you a copy, as required by law."

Emily was not deterred. She stared sweetly at the sheriff and waited patiently. She knew the sheriff wanted to get rid of her and considered sharing information with the press an obstacle to doing proper police work. She found a chair along the wall and sat down, making herself comfortable. She knew she was in for a considerable wait. A quick e-mail to Will would secure his patience, and she could work on the story while she waited. The coroner's report would change the lead, and the rest could already be written.

A couple of hours later, a police administrative clerk handed Emily a two-page report from the coroner, with a typed statement from Sheriff Dove Black at the very bottom. Emily realized that this was not the actual report, but the sheriff's summary. She called Will to start a Freedom of Information Request so they could get the actual report. That would be a story for another day. Meanwhile, with this official statement, Emily could write her story.

The next morning, people unfurled their paper to the following headline.

Coroner Says Wise County Man Died of Murder by Lethal Injection of the Wrong Drug
By Emily Scott

The story added that the sheriff's office would be "aggressively searching for Dr. Nicholas Oxenbriggs."

In his statement, the sheriff warned that finding Briggs would be challenging at best. No one knew for sure where he had gone. The sheriff added that Briggs was only a person of interest at this point.

A New Start

In a distant hospital, the anxious woman looked at her father, who seemed to get weaker by the day. He had once been a very strong iron worker, capable of scaling the heights of a skyscraper's skeletal frame. He had raised a large family, then lost two of his three children to the first Iraq War. His wife died of cancer a few years back, and his only remaining child, his beloved daughter, stood by him throughout his declining health. Now, she was leaning on this new doctor that everyone had been bragging about. Dr. Nicholas Briggs had been treating her father for about a week.

He had come to Port Luci, Louisiana just a few months earlier and had already built a loyal following. Patients said he stopped the clock when he met with a patient. He took all the time in the world. He listened, and he cared about his patients. But her father was now exhibiting some strange behavior. He apparently hallucinated and saw things that weren't real.

Dr. Briggs consoled her, telling her not to worry, that her father's condition would improve. So, she listened and took a break while her father slept.

Once he was sure the daughter had gone, Dr. Briggs slipped into the man's room. He stood over the bed for a moment, watching the man sleep. Then, he pulled a syringe from the breast pocket of his lab coat and deftly shoved its contents into a port on the IV tube that flowed into the man's arm.

"There, there. In a minute, you will be out of pain, at peace." Dr. Briggs softly said.

He watched the man convulse, then expel one last breath. Then, he fell still.

"Death is such a gift." Dr. Briggs said as he patted the man's arm and disappeared out into the corridor.

About the Author

Shadowed and protected by the mountains of her native southwest Virginia, Amelia Townsend has lived hither, thither, and yon—mostly between Virginia and North Carolina. She has worked as a newspaper and TV reporter, freelance producer and director, writer, and now PR hack. She is a proud graduate of the University of North Carolina at Chapel Hill.

She has no claim to fame. Further, she is most often bewildered when people say they are impressed by her work. Her first novel, *Keepsakes for the Heart*, was nominated by the N.C. Historical Association for the prestigious Ragan Old North State Award for non-fiction.

Her favorite avocation is listening to and writing down other people's stories, for truth surely is stranger and more beautiful than fiction. This is where Townsend has found fodder for the stories of the hills that she wrote with her late writing buddy. Several have come to life in the form of a novel and a couple of plays in production. The names have been changed to protect the guilty.

Townsend's most impressive accomplishments are her children—a son and daughter—who managed to turn in to fine young adults, despite her attempts to raise them.

Find her on:
Facebook: facebook.com/townsendart
LinkedIn: linkedin.com/ameliatownsend
Twitter: @townsendart
Website: shoestringtheatrecompany.com

Coming Soon

Coming up in the *Tall Tales from the Hills* series, *The Black Chamber*. This historical fiction book explores the facts and myths of Robert Townsend and Betty Blevins. He was a spy during the Revolutionary War. Betty lived during the Civil War, picking up her husband's rifle and marching into battle when he died. Yet somehow, Betty and Robert lived and loved together. It is a tale of subterfuge, intrigue, life and death, and two people who may have loved each other or maybe they never met.

CPSIA information can be obtained
at www.ICGtesting.com
Printed in the USA
JSHW010850171119
2477JS00001B/1

9 781950 895175